SHEPHERD'S SWORD

APOCALYPSE CHRONICLES

BOOK 4

DARREL SPARKMAN

ROUGH
EDGES
PRESS

Shepherd's Sword
Paperback Edition

Rough Edges Press
An Imprint of Wolfpack Publishing
9850 S. Maryland Parkway, Suite A-5 #323
Las Vegas, Nevada 89183

roughedgespress.com

This book is a work of fiction. Any references to historical events, real people or real places are used fictitiously. Other names, characters, places and events are products of the author's imagination, and any resemblance to actual events, places or persons, living or dead, is entirely coincidental.

Paperback ISBN 978-1-68549-296-0
eBook ISBN 978-1-68549-295-3
LCCN 2023937924

This is not an abstract future depicted in an apocalyptic novel.

It is not some future problem to be debated later.

Read the papers.

Listen to the news.

It is here.

The seeds are sown.

You are not ready.

SHEPHERD'S SWORD

ONE

ANNE WAS DEAD. And if he just had the guts to do it, so was he. Mason Law sat on the edge of the bed, staring out his bedroom window. His window. His bedroom now. His bed. No one to share it with. The one thing he had not prepared for, the one unthinkable thing in his life that he never thought about...had happened.

There was not much to see through the window, just the wind rustling silhouetted leaves bound to an oak that shrouded an amber streetlight; the window framed by the antique woodwork of the old farmhouse on the outskirts of Springfield, Missouri. The soft moaning of the wind gave credence to the storm slipping by.

He could hear the distant rumbling of thunder to the north, nothing unusual for April. Years of living in southwest Missouri before military service had taken over his life, told him that a thunderstorm to the north would be moving generally east and wouldn't be a factor. *No rain. No downburst of wind. No tornado. Who cares?*

The wood-framed farmhouse was bordered on three sides by a housing addition, but behind the house were pasture and a few animals. Other times he had been home, the field had been thick with cattle. Now there were none.

He looked at the framed picture on the dresser as his hand caressed the old model 1911 Colt .45 lying on the bed beside him. Anne. Anne, the compassionate. Anne, the faithful. Anne, of the unprepossessing love that allowed him to live his life as he wanted.

Anne, buried before he knew she had died. His eyes misted over. *Christ, where had the time gone?*

Both had agreed this was his last deployment. One last job. One last thing to do. They talked it over and knew things were winding down stateside. The economy was slowing, food and fuel shortages were commonplace, and Mason needed to be home. God knows he wanted to be.

For her part, Anne was learning everything she could about gardening, preserving their own food, and how to be self-sufficient in an entitlement world. They bought a generator and stored gasoline. Solar and wind generators would have been nice but were too expensive. There were many ways to try and ensure survival if you just had a lot of money. They both thought there would be enough time to prepare, that things would come apart more slowly. *More time.* Now the pantries had been gutted, the gasoline stolen, and the house had somehow turned into a lonely shell.

All the signs were there, of course—had been for years. No one was looking. Then, when time ran out, when all the pieces clicked together like cogs of some massive set of gears, it happened so quickly and easily it was almost anticlimactic. A lot of really smart people were standing around scratching their heads and asking, "What the hell just happened?"

Mason picked up the gun that had belonged to his father and before that, to his grandfather. His father had presented it to him when Mason had enlisted. He also presented him with a plaque that had a cross on it, entwined with deep-red roses growing from the base. It was inscribed, "Sometimes we die, that our father's blood be not shed in vain, that our children may walk freely upon this earth."

Typical of his father, he had used a permanent marker and attached a note in longhand. "Make sure it is the other guy that dies."

He hefted the gun in his hand. The old, original models were not accurate much beyond twenty-five yards. But he reckoned it would do well enough for this.

Sticking the barrel into his mouth, he grimaced and immediately took it out again. Gun oil. Why did he care? *C'mon, Mason.*

Standing in front of the bathroom mirror, he cleaned the barrel of the .45 with a towel. Looking at himself in the mirror, all he saw was average. With his job description, he had needed that. Brown hair, brown eyes, *haunted eyes*, and a face that could get lost in a crowd... and very frequently had.

Lean and tall. Skin tanned brown as a nut. Unremarkable as his lineage. He had so many nationalities in his family tree there was probably an alien or two in there somewhere. In fact, remembering one of his aunts, he was sure of it.

The mirror also showed a razor thin scar on the left side of his chest, nearly intersecting his nipple. Lower down, there were two dimples on his right side, right at about his belt line, with corresponding scars on his back. Jacketed shells from close range, or he wouldn't be here looking at it now. A chunk of meat missing from his right shoulder. He was proud all his wounds were in the front. Of course, there was that dimpled scar on his ass, but he wasn't telling anyone how he got that one.

What did he have to show for the last few years? Because of his deployments, he had been with Anne about half the time. Maybe less. No children, and she had been okay with that. Her parents were not thrilled about it, but they didn't like him anyway. *No chance, now.*

With the barrel of the gun cleaned to his satisfaction, he returned to the bed and sat. He knew he was depressed, and this was a coward's way out, that the guilt about not being there for Anne when she needed him was eating him up and pushing him to pull the trigger.

The shrinks would have a field day with his reasoning. Didn't matter. They wouldn't care, even if he had asked for help. It was too late. Nowhere to go…nothing to do…no one to do it with.

He experimented a moment with the muzzle at either temple. No. There were neighbors on either side, and the .45 slug would probably go through his house into the next, maybe into the next county. No, the angle had to be up.

Mason Law put the barrel of the .45 into his mouth, inverted and pointed upward, squeezed his eyes shut and pulled the trigger.

Nothing.

With a shuddering sigh, and a face suddenly wet with sweat, his hands dropped to his lap, holding the pistol. He stared at the offending pistol. How many times had he forgotten to thumb the safety off?

Eyes misting over, he fiercely squeezed them shut for a moment, and then with blurred vision stared at his trembling hands, lost in thought.

Close combat drill? Nope.

Targets and practice? Never.

Afghanistan? Not likely.

Iraq? Impossible, or he'd be dead.

Nicaragua, or South America; that little stint in North Africa? No. Not once. Nada.

Idiot.

He was not used to making mistakes. In his business, mistakes got you killed. Mistakes got other people killed. Mistakes were not tolerated. Ever.

With reproving eyes watching him from Anne's picture, he released the safety and raised the pistol.

I'm sorry, Anne. I should have been here. I should never have left you alone. All our plans...

The light in the room went out and it was dark as a well, ten feet down. Funny. He didn't feel a thing, and he could hear his shuddering breath and feel the bed he was sitting on. Mason envisioned hell as having a whole lot more light. Wouldn't the fires offer light? And, if this was Heaven, *unlikely*, where is the white light people had written about? Someone waiting for him, holding out their hand? *Wait...*

Mason sat for a moment. He didn't believe in ghosts, so he was reasonably sure Anne had not just killed the lights. Well, maybe he was sure.

Thumbing up the safety on the .45, he rose and stumbled into an exercise bike that he had surely passed by safely by a hundred times, found the window and looked outside. The neighborhood was dark in every direction he could see, only made darker by the occasional lightning show from the north. There was no glow or reflection in the sky from the city in the distance, so the power was out there, too.

Why? There was no storm here. No apparent cause. Somehow, he didn't think this was a brownout. The lights had not flickered, nor dimmed. He didn't know why, but it felt final.

Someone had thrown the big switch. And it was really, really dark. *What? You can't kill yourself in the dark?*

Huh. A guy can't even blow his brains out without something interfering.

Not that he needed an excuse to postpone the deed. It just was not working out. Bad karma.

Although he couldn't see it, he just knew Anne had winked at him from her picture.

Not your time, boy.

Not yet.

TWO

WILLARD TRASK, the Vice-President of the United States, stood gazing out a window. It was a small window, and the view was not spectacular. But he didn't expect it to be anything other than what it was because he was in a safe house—not the Capitol. The White House and Capitol grounds were not safe. Not anymore. The grounds were taken over by demonstrators, and instead of having the military fire on civilians, he had decided to vacate the premises and let them have it. Hell, it was the people's house anyway.

It was reported to him that thousands of people were now on the grounds and in the buildings. Even this place wouldn't be safe if anyone knew he was here. The populace was mad. And he was not sure if it was anger or mental disease. It would be easier to take if it was some sort of mass hysteria and not anger at the government. Now, a government he was responsible for.

The door to the room opened, and he turned his startled gaze to the newcomer, hoping his expression didn't show the indecision within him. Nothing in his life of public service to the people had prepared him for this. This nightmare.

Chief of Staff John Wells crossed the room and came up close, within whispering distance, and the vice-president moved back a pace. His personal space was about all he had left to protect anymore. Already in a bad mood, this irritated him even more. The atmosphere in the room had all the ambiance of a funeral parlor. Maybe that was fitting.

"I assume you've heard the news that POTUS is down?" John asked quietly.

"Yes, I have, Mr. Wells. Just a few minutes ago. It is unbelievable. With all the protection we have, I don't understand how an aircraft the size of Air Force One, plus the fighter escort with it, is destroyed." He paused for a moment, lost in thought.

Finally, he continued. "I am now the President. Given the circumstances, we'll clean up the paperwork later."

"That's alright, Mr. President. Congress is scattered to the four winds anyway, and I doubt there is a judge available anywhere to swear you in. I have prepared a simple document for you to sign stating that you are taking over the position and why. If the President should re-surface, then this will become null and void."

Willard Trask moved to his desk and with little flourish, signed the document to officially become President of the United States.

The next question from the chief of staff came softly. "Have you come to a decision yet?"

The President shook his head slowly. He didn't like this assistant any more than he supposed the assistant liked him. Still, he needed someone in the position. "Tell me one more time, Mr. Wells. Exactly what are we looking at? What are my advisers saying?"

"MR. PRESIDENT, when I was given this job, it was with the understanding that I would never pull any punches—that I would always be honest with the position of President, no matter who filled that position."

The President replied impatiently, "Yes, Mr. Wells. I understand. I understand that we don't like each other and that you don't agree with the things I do, or the policies that my party push forward."

John Wells sighed and took a nearby seat. He automatically crossed his legs, but could not stop his foot from doing a nervous bounce, so he put both feet on the floor. Taking a deep breath, he imagined he could smell the fresh spring air from outside instead of the stagnant processed air he was pulling into his lungs. The house was little more than a bunker, hardened against most known methods of attack.

Outside, it was the first week of April. The flowers were blooming, the birds were singing, and he didn't want to be inside this building staring at his shoes, trying to help someone he disliked so intensely.

"You asked what your advisers were saying. They are not saying much, because they are leaving in droves. That should be answer enough for you. As to the national situation, a few things have changed since the last briefing, sir."

John continued. "To summarize: Air Force One went down over Spain. No telemetry or voice messages were picked up. No GPS transponders are showing. It just disappeared. The fighter escorts disappeared also. We should at least entertain the idea that they defected to a country in less...shall we say, turmoil. There is no way of knowing currently. We may never know. But, even if that premise is true, it does not change the circumstances as far as your presidency is concerned. You are here. They are not.

"Congress is scattered with no means of coming back, even if they were so inclined. The simple answer is that the country is at a standstill. Quite literally. Politically as well as economically.

"As far as the reality of the situation. We are faced with a one-two punch, with various scenarios branching off from each, depending on locale. I don't suppose you have read the articles on the 'One Hour Meltdown' or the 'Hyperinflation Meltdown?'"

At the shake of the President's head, John started ticking off on his fingers, then seemed to realize he would run out of fingers before he stated the problems and folded his hands in his lap. "The first problem is fuel. With very few exceptions, like military stockpiles, we are tapped out across the country."

"But," the President interrupted, "we have more crude on the way. We made some concessions to the Chinese and Venezuelans. That is what the President was doing overseas. We just need a little time."

"Maybe that is why he disappeared. Maybe he didn't get any concessions. Anyway, it is too little, too late," John replied. "Any fuel being shipped will not get here in time to help most of the country."

The President said listlessly, "Our friends overseas..."

"Are not our friends. Never have been. They have

been telling us for years that they want us dead. We'll be lucky to avoid an invasion."

The President gazed angrily at his chief. "No one would dare. We are still the strongest country in the world. I still have launch capability and the strongest army on the earth."

"I disagree. And no matter how bad things are, I would be very leery of any humanitarian aid from Russia or China. They could put several hundred thousand troops on our soil by staging them through Cuba or Mexico, just to help us through our crisis of course, and they would never leave.

"One of the best deterrents to an invasion, one that other countries have admitted being true, is that over seventy percent of our populace is armed. However, starving people cannot be soldiers, and in a few days and weeks, they will be fighting each other for a few scraps of food. Nor will our military make rational decisions with their fingers on the trigger. Not if they are starving."

John watched the President grow angrier with each breath, wondering by his look which would come first—the heart attack or the stroke. Then he saw the quick anger leave his face and marveled at how easily the man changed moods. Willard Trask was a consummate politician through and through.

"How did you get to be my chief of staff if you disagree so much with all our policies? Why haven't you left with everyone else?" the President said. "Hell, I'm not even sure I have Secret Service anymore."

John said calmly. "Your protection detail is undermanned but still here. As to policy, although I may disagree with you on principle, none of that matters now.

You are the President. I'm here because I love my country."

The President gave his chief of staff a malevolent stare and then turned back to look out the window. "You may not believe this, but so do I, Mr. Wells. Now, what's the number two punch you mentioned?"

John stood again and paced the small room, cursing politicians who had no founding in either business or history. He thought of all the hours it would take to fully explain, of all the different ways to come to the inevitable conclusion. He settled for simplicity.

"Punch one and two are actually combined, like a good combination from a professional boxer, and I've already alluded to it. Number one was no fuel. Number two is no food, sir."

When the President turned and looked at him incredulously, John shrugged and said, "No fuel...no food. There is no way to transport it."

The President's face lost several shades of color and turned sickly pale. "That is impossible. We can surely move enough food around this country. What about airdrops or organizing distribution centers?"

John shook his head. "Distribution centers? FEMA couldn't handle a couple of hurricanes, much less a catastrophe of this magnitude. Besides, this has been going on for weeks. Months. Anyone warehousing food is tapped out. Even if you had a surplus of food, which you don't, you cannot put thousands of trucks on the road to deliver it. Not without fuel."

"I can't believe this. No one told us."

"That's because all your advisers are college professors. All their solutions are academic exercises on paper, and they wouldn't know a semi-truck from Noah's Ark."

"How much time do the people have?" the President asked.

John shook his head and replied in a voice made rough with emotion. "Depends on their locale. Some are feeling it already, but from the moment we stop making our military reserves available to the truckers, three days to a week. Some places will last longer, at least the people living in port cities will... Others will not last so long. Supermarkets and grocery stores in most cities re-supply every week, if not twice a week. A good amount of the trucks you usually see running up and down the Interstate on any given day are hauling food of one sort or another. Every morning, in front of every supermarket, you will normally see a truck waiting to unload frozen food, canned goods, bread, and perishables all waiting for the shelf."

"What about food banks?"

"Already tapped out and sucked dry. Any warehouse that had food has already been raided."

The President nodded. "I've seen the reports about rioting. I thought it was just regional. People mad about something. Hell, they are always mad about something. There are a ton of them sitting on the White House lawn right now."

"People are hungry, Mr. President. They don't give a damn about politics. Not now. It's the same in every city across the country, especially the major cities, but much worse in the Midwest."

The President looked at him. "Specifically?"

"The hardest hit is the area roughly west of the Mississippi and east of the Rockies. What you would call 'fly over country.' Although to be honest, the entire country is affected."

"Anything else?" the President asked peevishly. "Surely that's not all?"

John stopped pacing. "Most of the power grids are down. That means no communication. Cells are down, but SAT phones still work…for a while, anyway. Luckily, we are going into spring, so people won't need electricity for heat."

"How long before the grid is restored?"

The chief of staff looked at him incredulously for a moment, then finally found his voice. "Mr. President," he said softly. "It is not coming back. The only thing still producing is hydroelectric. Most of the city power plants in the country are coal-fired. Even if we started to mine coal again, we don't have any way to get it to the facilities."

"Wind power?"

"Localized. Always inefficient on a large scale."

"Nuclear?"

"Overloaded. Most have shut down."

"How long before a re-start up?"

John rolled his eyes, glad the President was not looking at him. "Weeks? Months? Hell, I don't know."

"What about buying power from Canada or Mexico?"

"Not possible. Besides, they have their own set of problems."

"How many?"

John looked puzzled. "Sir?"

"How many people will we lose? How many will die?"

Unable to meet the President's gaze, John replied, "The only thing that allows our country to support its population is available energy and technology. Loss of life will be horrendous, even in the parts of the country we still control. In the Midwest?" He shrugged. "Half the populace? Maybe more. I just don't know."

The freshly minted President of the United States was silent for a long moment, then walked slowly into an adjoining bathroom and threw up.

After returning, he calmly said, "Bring in my general."

THE PRESIDENT'S general was Nathan Ferguson, a politically savvy up and comer that had been selected over more seasoned officers for his propensity to agree with the administration. Although the President didn't own him, it was close enough.

With General Ferguson and Chief of Staff Wells seated, the President turned to them.

"This is the hardest decision I've ever made. There is a medical term called triage, which basically means saving what you can and letting the rest go. It is my belief, and regret, that we have to triage our country. This is the only way I can see to move forward at this time. If we try to save everyone, the country will fall. And, gentlemen, we may lose part of it, but we will not lose this country."

"General," the President continued. "I want you to give orders to activate all units, regular, reserve, and National Guard. Anybody and everybody. All federal employees, all of the alphabet agencies like FBI and CIA, from the top on down, will be under our joint command. Is that understood?"

General Ferguson said, "Yes, sir."

John Wells just sat with his mouth open.

"We will declare martial law immediately. Also, if there is any way to get them here, pull in what overseas assets we have to help with controlling the populace and guard our borders. We will concentrate on the east and west coast. That is where our largest population centers are. We will divert any available power and stores to the coasts. No military or civilian supplies of fuel will cross the Mississippi River or the Rockies. All military personnel not involved in direct control of the populace will be pulled out of the middle of the country and positioned on the east side of the Mississippi River."

"It is unfortunate," the President continued. "Actually horrendous. But we must cut the middle of the country loose. From this moment on...they are on their own."

The General spoke for the first time. "That will be a death trap for the civilians, sir. The people will not stand for it. They are facing starvation. If we start packing people into the cities with little food, water, or medical care...the death toll will be tremendous. Also, I'm not sure I can hold all of our guard units. Maybe not even the regulars under that scenario."

The President exploded at his general. "We have had the NorthCom plan in place since we brought home hardened troops from Iraq and Afghanistan, just for this contingency. You are telling me now that we don't control our own military units?"

"There is that possibility, sir," the General replied calmly. "Also, this is not like any other place in the world. The populace is armed and nearly as well as the government, not counting heavy arms and aircraft, of course. They could organize and head for the coasts and borders. If we try to stop them, we could have a bloodbath on our hands."

"General, it is up to you to hold the units in place. Desertions cannot be tolerated. Anything less than full loyalty will not be acceptable. Standing order number one, General. We must control the populace. They will be contained until the crisis is over, by whatever means is necessary. We cannot have another revolution in this country. There will be no news, no blogging or tweeting. You will shut down the internet immediately, if it is even operating. Satellite communication will be blocked and used by the military only. The world must not realize just how weak we are. Is that clear?"

"What about people living outside the cities? And possible rogue units on one side and armed militia on the other?" the General asked.

"That will be up to the commanders in the field. You should make an effort to bring everyone into the cities. It is easier to control them there."

"And if they refuse?"

"According to our constitution, everyone has a right to bear arms and to have an armed militia. It is also their right to die for their conviction. My orders are *by any means necessary*, General. The 'means' are up to the commander in the field."

There was little else to discuss. The underlings in the chain of command would handle the minutia. The General, his face ashen and aged another twenty years, left to see if he had a chain of command left.

The President turned to his chief of staff. "I need a press release done."

John Wells laughed before he could stop himself. "A press release to whom, sir? Who will you be talking to? There is no electricity in most of the country, so there is no communication other than military. No internet. No

Facebook or Twitter. No online news. For once, the people will have to make up their own minds with the information at hand and what they see—not what is handed to them by a thirty-second sound bite."

"Mr. Wells, I don't want this. No one would want this. None of this could be anticipated."

"That is incorrect, sir. It has been staring us in the face for a long time."

The President pinned John with his gaze for a long moment, then said, "Three weeks is not a very long tenure for a chief of staff."

"Longer than the tenure of the last half dozen," John said with a smile, knowing he was one of the last to leave the sinking ship.

The President's voice softened and was calm and measured. "You are fired, go home and take care of your family."

"Thank you, sir." John Wells turned and followed the General's path from the room. He turned at the door, but the President was gazing out the window again. Former Chief of Staff John Wells left his shrinking government, already thinking of how to get home, how to convince his wife they should leave immediately and get the family to their cabin, how to keep them safe, how to quell the hungry grumbling in his belly, details...details. And simultaneously feeling relief and guilt for being fortunate enough to live on the East Coast.

THREE

DAYLIGHT and the dawning of a new day can do strange things to your mind. Somehow, death didn't seem so palatable when Mason breathed the fresh air of the morning, heard the birds singing and dogs barking.

He drove slowly into Springfield, Missouri, from the north, heading down Glenstone Avenue toward the Great Southern bank just a few blocks from the I-44 interchange. The Dodge Ram Sport pickup grumbled along, the very sound bragging power and strength. With the gas this thing used, he hoped he would have enough to get back home. Funny, the last he knew, the tank was full. He would have to talk to his next-door neighbor about that. Admiral Holloway, retired, kept a weather eye on everything.

As he drove, his thoughts were on last night. If he had succeeded in pulling the trigger and gone to meet Anne—he could not bring himself to call it suicide—he was sure she would have kicked his butt. Anne could not stand a quitter. *Then how did she die so quickly? Didn't she fight for life?*

Last night would have been a terrible mistake. He would have looked down at his body and said, "You dumb shit, why in the hell did you do that?" St. Peter would have shrugged his shoulders and said, "Beats me."

He put the whole thing down to grief and mental fatigue. And he didn't get a chance to say goodbye, never got to see her. She was just gone.

AFTER SNATCHING his package from an armed camp—the package being an informer that had been caught—he delivered the man to his commanding officer. Not that he cared about one snitch, but he was our spy and the powers that be who ruled his world wanted him back safely.

Mason's commanding officer shook his hand and congratulated him on a job well done under more than hazardous conditions. He then bluntly told him that his wife was dead and he was being sent back to the States. He was told that because of his service to his country, no expense would be spared to get him home. His last instructions were chilling.

"Son," the commander said, "as soon as you have things squared away at home, your orders are to report to General Slade at Fort Leonard Wood. That is the official line. Privately, my advice is this—no paperwork will follow you, but consider yourself discharged of your duties. Considering the way things are stateside, I wouldn't leave the Springfield area. Get your affairs in order. Keep your head on a swivel and your shit wired tight. I have it on good authority that things back home are coming apart. When that happens, it is going to get ugly in a hurry."

With that, the man stood from his desk and first saluted Mason, and then shook his hand. "That is all, soldier. Godspeed."

Mason remembered the whirlwind connection of flights that had brought him up from Central America to deposit him in Fort Hood, Texas, flights that had afforded little sleep...and the mind-numbing fact that his wife had died weeks before, and he would never see her again.

THE ELECTRICITY HAD COME BACK on this morning but was feeble and flickering, and wouldn't even heat up his toaster. That is, if he'd had any bread. But he made do. A cold can of ravioli in scrumptious tomato sauce was not his first choice for breakfast, but what the hell?

His thought when he hit the road was to clean out their safe deposit box and close out their checking account. To be honest, he didn't know how much was in the account. Anne had always taken care of such things for them. Anne...*dammit, Anne. Why am I mad at you for dying? How stupid is that?*

Mason could not remember ever being depressed, didn't know the definition of the term depression. Maybe this was it. The big empty. Nobody home. He used to care about things, but now he just didn't care at all. There wasn't anything that interested him. Not with Anne gone. And now the anger. Why was he so damned mad?

He finally got a break in traffic and whipped into the shared drive between the bank and the Oasis Convention

Center, narrowly missing a line of people in the parking lot. There was a crowd of people at both the front and back door of the bank. Would-be customers were shaking the locked doors while others were picking up rocks from the landscaping next to the road and throwing them at the windows. Inside the bank, the security guard and a couple of suits flinched every time a rock hit the window.

Mason lowered his driver-side window and spoke to a man standing near him. The man was dressed in a dark suit and stood idly with his hands in his pockets.

"I take it the bank is closed?" Mason asked.

"Yeah," the man replied in a relaxed manner, as if he were watching the 'big game' on television. "Apparently, as soon as people tried to withdraw money, the guards kicked everyone out and locked up. ATMs are locked up everywhere...no internet...it's that way all over town. Stores can't use debit or credit cards, has to be cash only. Which is kind of funny. Look around you. Everyone wants their money, but what do you think a dollar will buy you right now? Absolutely nothing. Everything just shut down all at once, like someone threw a big switch somewhere. Even cell phones are down. It is the strangest thing I have ever seen."

Mason came out of his self-imposed fog and sat up straight in the pickup seat. What is the first thing a government must do in the face of growing unrest from the people? Stop communication. So no internet and no telephone. Next would be to freeze assets. No money could be moved, even though it was not worth much. If all the banks were closed and electricity spotty or gone, then the vaults were locked and not likely to open. Even if someone broke into a bank, their gold, silver, and jewelry—things they could use for barter currency—were unavailable. If you run to the market for a jug of milk, your cash money is not worth much, your credit or debit card will not work, and the store is probably closed anyway because the cash registers are not working. What to do?

He could see it all around him. People looked mad, scared, and desperate. The government, whether it be federal, state, or local, would be the cause of the very scenario they were trying to avoid. Things were going to get broken. A lot of things.

As he sat pondering the situation, a growing crowd packed the streets. How had he missed that? From his vantage point, it looked like all the fast-food places and restaurants within sight had closed, and there were a lot of them in this area. The businesses were being reopened with anything that could be tossed through a window. Strangely enough, the parking lots were filling with people and cars. If you had gas for your vehicle, wouldn't it be better to save it for an emergency? But then, here he sat—burning gas.

He started his truck and drove slowly on south through the parking lot connecting all the businesses in this strip with the Walmart store—Wally World to the locals—right around the corner to the east. When he turned the corner, having passed the abandoned Quik Stop gas pumps and the backlot of a café, he braked to a stop. The parking lot of the Walmart Super Center was jammed with vehicles and people. The huge crowd in the lot reminded him of video he had seen once on the news of soccer games in Europe when the home team lost. These people were not happy, pushing and shoving each other in an effort to reach the doors of the superstore.

Mason's fingers caressed the .45 lying on the seat next

to him, thinking of fighting his way into the store to see if anything remained that was useful.

Nope. It was not worth it. He had a pretty good supply of stuff at home. Hell with it...he'd had enough of fighting and killing.

As he watched, he saw a group of men carrying gas cans going methodically from vehicle to vehicle with a small hand pump, and emptying every tank they came to. There were men in charge of carrying the cans, one doing the pumping, and several men with rifles standing guard. One SUV they came to had people in it. When the occupants got out of the vehicle to try and stop the gas thieves, they were pummeled to the ground.

He turned the truck around and headed north. Time to get outta Dodge.

FOUR

JENNIFER BOUDREAUX SLIPPED into the Walmart store through a jam-packed entryway and navigated slowly through the mass of people, surprised and pleased the lights were on and checkout registers working. She guessed as long as there was electricity, the store would try and make a buck. It looked to her as if once the mob of people got through the bottleneck at the doors and into the store, they had little idea what they wanted to do. Most were just running up and down the aisles. She could see that the biggest crowds were in the grocery section, and on the opposite side of the store, the sporting goods.

Having left home in a hurry, she was dressed in a tank top, cutoff jeans, and flip-flops for the warm spring day. Her dishwater-blonde hair was pulled through the back of a Cardinal's ball cap into a ponytail. She grabbed a cart, feeling lucky to find one and double lucky for making it out of the parking lot and into the store alive. It was unbelievable to her that she had found the courage to not turn and run.

The parking lot of the store at Kearny and Glenstone looked like a demolition derby on crack cocaine. Everyone was moving at a frantic pace and had apparently left their driving skills at home. A transplanted New Orleans native, Jennifer could not decide if the chaos in the store reminded her of pre-Katrina, or post-Katrina. Or maybe some B-grade disaster movie. It was hard to imagine what the south part of Springfield looked like since there were more people living there. As the overhead lights blinked off and on a few times and then stayed on, she laughed to herself. This was nuts! She could not imagine all the stories they would have to tell when it was all over.

People were rushing through the store in waves, much like she had seen birds in flight changing direction instantly, en masse. There were men, of course, but she was surprised to see women and children, some holding babies...all running up and down the aisles trashing things on their way. Some would pull things off the shelves, and others would just stomp on them. Then, there were people like her that would try to pick up things they needed.

Peeking down an aisle and finding it relatively clear of people-jam, she steered her cart toward the diaper and baby needs, dodging discarded clothes littering the aisle floor. The clothes kept getting tangled in the wheels of the cart. She was out of Pampers for the baby. Her younger sister was babysitting at home. The only reason Jennifer came here today was that, for damn sure, she was not going back to washing diapers in the toilet like her mom had told her about. Yuck!

Pulling the last two packages off the shelf and not caring what size they were, she flinched as incredibly loud gunfire erupted, and people started screaming a few aisles over. The sound of people running, their shoes slapping on the tile floor, coupled with the smell of what she supposed was gunpowder, stopped her in her tracks. Then she was horrified as she saw blood running under the display counter from the next aisle over.

This is bad! Get out!

Putting her head down and trying to ignore a cold knot of fear in her stomach, she hurried toward the coolers to see if there might be milk or juice left.

Jennifer never saw what abruptly stopped her cart, slamming the handle into her belly. Stunned for a moment and trying to catch her breath, she looked up to see three men standing around her. As she watched them stare at her, she became acutely aware of the low-cut tank top she had chosen to wear. The men were just looking at her, smiling. She suddenly felt naked. When she shivered, she knew it was from fear, not cold.

"Please," she pleaded with them, shaking her head. It didn't take a genius to know what they wanted. "I have kids at home. Please don't hurt me. Let me go."

The tallest man, wearing a wife-beater tee shirt to show off arms covered in tattoos, cut-off jeans, and, incongruously, boots, grabbed her by the arm.

"I think this'un will work just fine, don't you boys? Let's take her out to the camper."

When they didn't respond to her pleas, Jennifer tried to break free, but two of the men grabbed her by the arms and started dragging her toward the front doors as she kicked out at them. Her screams blended in nicely with the other screams in the store as she struggled to get away. When the group neared the front entrance, she nearly broke free, but a large fist knocked her sprawling into a magazine rack. The headlines leaped out at her as she struggled to regain her senses: Rioting in major cities! St. Louis, Kansas City, Detroit, Los Angeles...

A man leaped out of the crowd and pushed the men off her. While the good Samaritan was bent over her, one of the assailants pulled a revolver from under his shirt and shot the man point blank in the back. Jennifer jerked as she felt a searing pain in her side and was simultaneously showered in blood. The man fell on top of her. She tried to push the body off her, but weakness came quickly, and her hands fell away.

Her last thoughts before she blacked out were, *My babies...what will happen...?*

AMY WAS one of the girls running the checkout register closest to the shooting and had never been so afraid in her life. She looked at the woman sprawled under the dead man, seeing her feeble attempts to push the man away while watching the blood spread on the tile floor. Even as she watched, one of the men who shot the woman lying in front of her pointed at another girl in the crowd trying to make her way out the door. She could see the woman throwing frightened glances over her shoulder at the men rushing toward her as she pushed and shoved her way out the door. The three men following her were laughing as they followed.

She was startled again as she heard the woman lying under the sprawled body of the man who had tried to help her, muttering something about babies.

Amy turned and said to her friend Marcie at the next register, "We better call 9-1-1. This place is going crazy."

"You're kidding, right?" Marcie replied. "I've seen a dozen cops in this crowd already. Ain't nobody answering at 9-1-1. Besides, last time I checked, the phone didn't work. That's why we're supposed to be doing cash only. No outside phone lines and no internet."

Both girls looked down the line of checkout stations to see hardly any checkers were still there. They looked at the sea of people surrounding them for a moment, then at each other. The sound of so many voices yelling and screaming was getting louder by the minute.

Amy yelled, "Any reason we're still here?"

Marcie was already stuffing money from the cash drawer of her register into her pockets. "Oh, hell no," she replied. "We should have left the first time we heard shots. The manager told us to stay, but I ain't seen his ass in over an hour. We're outta here."

Hundreds of people were pushing and shoving to get out of the store, holding bags and packages. The people streaming into the doors decided it was easier to steal from the people in front of them instead of battling to get into the store, and the crowd started fighting. Gunfire erupted in the middle of the crowd and panicked people bolted in all directions, trying to get away, trampling anyone who might trip and fall in front of them.

Amy and Marcie broke away and ran for a side entrance. Ignoring the sign on the door that said 'Alarm will sound if this door is used—door will open in fifteen seconds after the handle is pushed,' they hammered and pushed against the door until it opened and added the loud squeal of the subsequent alarm to the cacophony of sound coming from behind them. Part of the crowd of shoppers, looters now, pushed out of the doors with them.

When they stumbled outside, the girls saw the parking lot was jammed with people and cars. As far as they could see, the streets were clogged like blocked arteries and nothing was moving. It looked like everyone in Springfield had hit the road at once. They could see that nothing on wheels was going to move, so the girls started walking.

So did everyone else.

Some carried groceries or bags of clothes, but most were empty-handed...until they fought for someone else's groceries.

"Where we goin'?" Amy asked, shaking her head in wonder as a gang-banger ran down the street carrying a big flat-screen television. He was dressed in low-slung jeans and a sleeveless hoodie. It was almost comical as the teenager tried to keep up his pants with one hand while holding the television with the other and still run.

Amy pointed at the guy and said, "Maybe there should be an Olympic event for that?"

"Yeah, like there will be an Olympics anymore," Marcie replied.

"So, where do you want to go?"

"Back to the apartment, I guess. Score some of the food I've been laying by. Hang out," Marcie said. "We will have to come back for the car later, although I'm betting all the gas will be gone from it."

Amy's voice was trembling. "Yeah, I think we can forget the car. It's a piece of junk, anyway. Then what?"

"I don't know. We'll ask the guys when they show up. I think we need to get out of town, away from these crowds, but I don't know where to go or what direction. I just don't know..."

"Do you think the guys will show up?"

Marcie snickered. "They're guys. We have food and benefits. They'll come."

"That's what I'm afraid of. We should have grabbed more condoms before we left. If we get pregnant now…"

Marcie laughed. "Great. Most people are stealing food and water. You want to steal condoms."

"Look, I'm scared, Marcie. Okay? I just don't know what to do or what we need. We both missed Survival 101 class in school."

Holding Amy's hand, Marcie looked around at the utter chaos around them and said, "I'm scared, too, Amy. We just need to go with the flow and wait. Someone will take charge of this, straighten everything out, and then we'll get help."

JENNIFER BOUDREAUX FELT weak and could hardly breathe. Although she could not see anything around her, she could hear sounds—sounds that made her want to go back to sleep or just hide away. She could hear running footsteps and the sound of things being thrown on the floor. Mixed with those sounds were screaming, shouting, and strangely enough, laughter. The weight on top of her kept crushing her down. She felt so tired. Maybe she could just rest some more.

My babies! The thought went crashing through her mind and she shook her head to clear her mind. Memories of what had happened to her came flooding back, and she started desperately squirming under the weight of the body on her. The smell was awful. She had read once that when someone dies, their bladder and bowels let loose, and she could smell that all around her. Frantic now, she soon worked one arm out from under the body. Shoving and wiggling, she finally got the weight off her. But she still could not see.

Frantically, both hands went to her eyes, and she discovered her face was covered with a sticky substance. Carefully, she wiped her eyes until she could open them and see—and then wished she had not. She was covered in blood. Looking at the man that had fallen on her, it looked like he had lived long enough to bleed out all over her and the floor. Her side was throbbing, and she quickly discovered she had a searing burn along her abdomen. She guessed some of the blood was hers after all.

When she remembered how the man had tried to help her, and then she thought of the three men who were abducting her, one hand went to her crotch, and she was relieved her pants were still on. Thank God!

Finally, rolling to her hands and knees, she stood. Leaning against the counter next to her, she looked around and thought of earthquake pictures she had seen on television. The store was in complete shambles. It didn't bother her that she had been left for dead. She was grateful.

On shaking legs and taking tentative steps, she went out the wide front doors of the building to head home. There were bodies out by the door on the sidewalk. As she looked at them, there was no doubt in her mind they were dead. Very dead. It looked like they had been stomped to death. When she remembered the huge mob of people trying to get into the store, she had no doubt as to how they died.

As she headed south, crossing Kearny Street, she met a few people that gave her a wide berth. She knew why.

Covered in blood, she also stank from the body that had emptied out on top of her. A fleeting thought came to her. She imagined that she looked like one of those zombies there were so many television series about.

It was nearly dark when she finally stumbled up her street to the little duplex they lived in. The door was hanging on one hinge and the windows were broken out.

"No!" Her anguished cry echoed off the building front. A quick look revealed the adjoining apartment was in the same shape. With her hand to her mouth to keep from crying, she edged into the house. The place had been torn apart. Trying to call out, she could not find her voice. Frantic, she quickly looked in all the rooms and found no one. The kitchen was ransacked, and all the food except spices and condiments was gone. Nothing edible was left.

Her babies! Her little sister! Her husband should have been home by now. Where was he?

Jennifer Boudreaux collapsed onto the living room floor. She tried to cry, but nothing came out. On some level, she knew it was shock, but the knowledge didn't help. Her world had been torn apart in a way she had never dreamed would happen. She was not prepared. No one she knew would be prepared. How could they? Her only hope was that there were no bodies, and she prayed her family got away. But to where? Where could they go?

Then she saw a little bootie sock lying on the floor. Just one. White with two pink stripes around the top. One of her little girls had been wearing it when she left. Picking it up, she held it to her nose, then against her eyes. As full darkness settled on the quiet neighborhood, Jennifer sat in the middle of a house that looked like the store she had left. Shambles. She wept.

FIVE

THE TRIP to the bank had been fruitless in one sense and educational in another. Dodging cars and people made the drive back tedious and slow. If Mason had not been almost out of town when he started, he might not have made it through the congestion. It took all his concentration to keep from running over people, or getting hit by insane drivers. He even saw people fighting at gas pumps, when everyone knew there was no gas, and flinched when he heard shots fired. Mason thought that the gas pumps had run dry days ago. Exhausted when he finally got home, he laid down on the bed to rest and the next thing he knew, it was dark.

He flipped on the light switch and headed for the end table where his Colt rested. That was as far as he got before the lights went out again.

From the bedroom window, Mason glanced up and down the street, could not see a thing, and then raised his shirttail and tucked the Colt behind his waistband.

Outside, it was dark in only the way it can be when someone is used to seeing light all the time...somewhere.

Close in, or lights in the distance, there always seems to be light—and light being a sign of civilization and the instant feelings of not being alone comes with it. He had experienced this kind of darkness before, but that was deep in the jungle.

After walking into the exercise bike, bruising his shin and ramming the handlebar into his crotch, he marveled at his lack of short-term memory as he rummaged in the nightstand for his mini Maglite. He turned it on and condensed the world to a tight illuminated beam and then went out the bedroom door toward the front of the house.

When he stepped out the front door, it looked like a *Star Wars* fight with the Jedi Knights assailing the forces of evil with their lightsabers, but it was only his neighbor's flashlight beams waving around the neighborhood, lighting up things they had already seen thousands of times earlier. One neighbor had a light bright enough to be measured in megawatts and was better suited for lighting up the Empire State Building trying to find King Kong. In the distance, he could see a new glow over the city. Mason was sure this glow came from a fire, and a big one...maybe two or three fires. That was one way to turn the lights back on. Effective, until you run out of fuel.

Mason saw his neighbor on the right start to trot over, the glow of his flashlight bouncing with every step.

"Watch out for that..."

The neighbor tripped, and with a curse, went ass over teakettle into the lawn, his flashlight bouncing toward Mason.

"...trellis wire," Mason said mildly as he bent to pick up the now broken cheap plastic flashlight.

Admiral Charles K. Holloway limped up to him and

snatched the light out of his hand, then proceeded to slap it against his own palm, trying to get it to come on.

"I think your lightsaber is broken," Mason commented.

"What?"

Mason guessed the Admiral was not a *Star Wars* fan.

Holloway slapped the offending flashlight a few more times. "Law, you owe me a flashlight."

"The hell I do. You're trespassing. If I'd known you were coming, I could have set the grass on fire to light the path. That way, you wouldn't have tripped."

"Trespassing? Why, I've been mowing your lawn for... well—" He stammered to a stop.

Mason sighed. "I know, since Anne died."

When he thought of the night before up in the bedroom, the memory was already becoming faint. "Still, you should have remembered the trellis wire."

They both stood in silence a moment, both uncomfortable with the memory of Mason's wife.

IT HAD BEEN a few weeks ago when he walked out of triple canopy jungle and heard his wife had died. His commanding officer immediately put him on leave and arranged a flight home, and flights were hard to come by. Mason was surprised because fuel of any kind was scarce for the military, and nearly non-existent for the public. But there seemed to be a lot of traffic inbound to the States. Through a combination of flights, he had arrived in Fort Hood, Texas. There was no gas to spare for motor transport, so Mason had done the next best thing, and hopped another flight.

Mason thought of the flight going from Fort Hood in Texas to Fort Leonard Wood, just up I-44 from Springfield, Missouri. He was reasonably sure the plane had landed at its destination. He just had not been with it. While flying over the north side of Springfield, a little money had passed to the pilots; and he had stepped out of a perfectly good airplane. It was a testament to the pilots that upon his request, they had only asked 'about where' he would like to land. They had come down to five thousand feet, opened the cargo door, and Mason had stepped out. The only witnesses to that were the flight engineer (again, more money) and several startled military passengers sitting on the side benches.

On his way past the jump seats that were full of personnel bound for Fort Leonard Wood, a grizzled sergeant commented, "Goin' for a walk?"

"Beautiful day in the Ozarks, Sarge. I'm actually doing a snap inspection and 'quality control' checks on parachutes."

"You don't say? Well, everyone's gotta have a job." The soldier leaned back and closed his eyes. "If that one does not work, try and hit the ground perpendicularly. If you go in like a yard dart, it is a lot easier to clean up."

After the soldier's comment, Mason was elated when the chute opened. He made a decent landing in a pasture, narrowly missing someone's milk cow, several cow patties, well, all but one, and a herd of goats. The cow continued chewing her cud, like someone dropping out of the sky was an everyday occurrence. Luckily, the Jersey cow was not wearing his chute for a hat and dragging him all over hell's half-acre.

———

HOLLOWAY CLEARED HIS THROAT. "Sorry about Anne. Hell of a thing, losing her that way."

Mason shrugged, glad it was dark so the Admiral could not read his expression. Or see his eyes. "There is a lot of dying going on, I guess."

"Yes, there certainly has been." Holloway cleared his throat again and then spoke sharply. "You armed?"

Startled, Mason switched on his light for about a half-second and painted Holloway's face, and then switched it off.

"Jesus!" Holloway said as his hands came up to ward off the blinding light.

Mason thought about telling the Admiral how he had already saved his life by not shooting toward his house the evening before but restrained himself. "Sorry. I just wondered if you were serious."

The Admiral was rubbing his eyes. "I think I'm blind. Hell, I know I'm blind. That was a stupid, amateur trick. And, damn straight, I am serious. We've had a lot of looting lately."

"Toasters and blenders?" Mason asked lightly, thinking of the power being out and some crackhead trying to fence an electrical appliance at a local pawnshop.

"Guns and food, smart-ass. Any kind of ammo. But, mostly food."

Mason Law gazed toward the darkened city. He was sure one of the fires burned in downtown Springfield.

"Is the fire department still running?" he asked.

The Admiral snorted. "Sure. All they have to do is push the tanker trucks to the fire, then get some gerbils to spin the wheel that is hooked to the pump—"

Mason interrupted. "Yeah, yeah. I got it."

"So, it's starting," Mason continued. "We had an Intel briefing several months ago about this very thing, that things were winding down stateside and we would have to be careful. I thought we would have more time."

Mason shook his head, thinking that everyone always thinks there will be more time. He turned on the mini-mag with the beam pointing down. "Here ya go, Admiral." Holding the light out to the man, he said, "It's all yours."

"Thanks." Admiral Holloway took the flashlight. "All I can see when I close my eyes is a big white dot. I may be blinded for the rest of my life, short as it might be." Holloway put his hand on Mason's arm. "If you hear something go 'boom' in the night, don't come running over. I can't tell the saints from the sinners in the dark."

"I'll try and restrain myself," Mason said.

After the Admiral slowly returned to his house, Mason started to go back inside and then thought better of it. It would be hot inside, and he hated the thought of the confining house. He pulled a folding deck chair off the porch and set it on the sidewalk. It was a nice spring evening, just right for camping out.

Adjusting the .45 to a better position and thinking he would have to change his arsenal soon, Mason sat and watched the light show in the city. The fire was growing larger and he could faintly hear occasional gunshots and explosions. He could not hear the screams of fear and anger, but had enough experience to know it was happening. It was the land of the free, home of the brave—and there was probably more ordinance over there than on a military base.

Just me and the skeeters, waiting to see what goes

bump in the night. He sighed. *Hell, I got nothing better to do.*

MASON CAT-NAPPED until the early hours of the morning. He was wide awake when he heard them coming. They were not trying to hide and not even trying to be quiet, their shadows and silhouettes looking like a motley band of adult ragamuffins marching down the middle of the street, an odd assortment in hoodies and baggy pants. By the light of a waning moon, it looked like they had long guns—rifles, or shotguns, judging by the obvious way they carried them—and maybe some sticks or canes and a lot of useless swagger.

When the gang stopped in front of the Admiral's house, Mason extricated himself from the lawn chair and eased over against the side of his house for the slight cover it would afford.

"You boys move along," he said loudly. "There are easier pickin's farther down the road."

When he spoke, the group flinched as one and seemed to move as one large shadow, like a dark oil slick on water. He was sure a couple of them nearly had heart attacks, judging by their audible gasps. By the smell, one had surely watered his shoes. Mason reasoned that this was just a group of boys out prospecting, trying to be men and dealing with their fear the only way they knew how. Their fathers probably didn't know how either. A few of them may have been in gangs, but he would bet they were not hardcore because he was not dodging lead by now. Some had probably stolen their father's guns. They were not hungry enough nor desperate enough to be very dangerous. Not yet. But, he reasoned, this was going on all over town and also knew it wouldn't take long for the confrontations to get ugly.

One enterprising soul wanting to be the alpha male replied loudly, "We go where we want. Now, why don't you come out here where we can see you and maybe we won't kill your sorry ass!"

Mason chuckled. *Now why in the hell would I do that?* Not a soldier among them, or they would know how vulnerable they were all bunched up.

"Not likely," he said.

One of the shadows moved as if he might raise his weapon, and Mason instantly fired one shot over their heads. The thing about a .45, if the low-velocity bullet didn't kill you, the noise would. It is loud beyond description and on a still night...and, with nerves on edge?

The muzzle flash painted their startled faces and left Mason with ruined night vision and ringing in his ears.

Over the fading echoes of the gunshot, he distinctly heard the sound of something falling in the Admiral's house, a shotgun blast, and then muffled cursing.

"Next time," he said sharply to the group, "someone dies. Now, back off."

Without a spoken word, the members located at the back of the group started drifting away, leaving only those in front who felt a need to show they were unafraid. Mason didn't say anything else, letting the silence work on them, and in a minute flat, the street was empty.

Mason heard the Admiral's door ease open and saw him walking over, studiously avoiding the trellis wire.

"I heard a noise," the Admiral said gruffly.

"Yeah, me, too," Mason replied, glad the Admiral

could not see his grin. "Maybe I fell out of the lawn chair and my gun went off. It could have happened to anyone, I suppose. You know how it is, waiting for marauding toaster thieves and such. Then you accidentally go to sleep on watch. Next thing you know, you are surrounded by the bad guys, gunshots everywhere. I'll try to be more careful next time."

"You do that, Law." The Admiral stood looking up the street. Dawn was still an hour away, so Mason knew he could not see much.

"Try to hold the noise down, will ya. People are trying to sleep around here," the Admiral said gruffly as he walked away a few steps and then turned. "And I didn't fall."

"Of course not." Mason chuckled as he watched the man walk away. "Hey, Admiral. You need help fixing your drywall?"

"Shut up."

"Right." Mason sighed and then chuckled as he shook his head, trying to clear his ears of the ringing. Yeah, Anne was right. Life was better. It was good to be alive.

SIX

MAJOR GENERAL MATTHEW SLADE sat at his desk in the administration building at Fort Leonard Wood, Missouri. He had just received a report from Jefferson Barracks via SATCOM that the St. Louis area was in complete riot, and the Army post on the south side of St. Louis was about to be overrun. The Air Wing had evacuated all their aircraft that would fly, but the ground pounders were left to their own devices. Huge gangs of people were ransacking everything they came to. The loss of life was already horrendous. People were fleeing the city. The communication tech he had talked to said he used the term gang loosely. When people thought of gangs as usually more than three and less than twenty, he was talking hundreds of people, if not thousands. There was no way to get an accurate count. He had heard that the Missouri Highway Patrol had abandoned their vehicles because they ran out of gas, and the roads were full of people, so they could not drive. The people didn't know where they were going but were just going. Some were calling them refugees. Most were calling them movers or raiders because that was exactly what the people were doing.

The community surrounding Fort Leonard Wood was holding it together so far, but that was largely because most of the people were military or their dependents. Another report came in that Interstate 44, between St. Louis and just east of Fort Leonard Wood, was completely jammed. Not with vehicles but with people. Hundreds of thousands of people, and they were headed his way. *Where were they going?* He had used precious fuel and launched a helicopter to confirm this, but it had not returned and was overdue. He didn't know if they had mechanical problems, or if the crew had just kept on going.

His first order was to send several sapper units east in an attempt to blow the bridges across a couple of the deep gorges. After all, this was an ordinance training facility. With the topography of the area, that alone would impede progress and buy him some time.

The second order, after hearing of the mass exodus, was to order all personnel and their dependents onto the grounds of the Fort. The area of Fort Leonard Wood was huge, but if he could pull everyone back to a defensible position, it might work. It was better than running. Sirens were going off everywhere as emergency vehicles sped into the surrounding community to spread the word. He didn't know if he could save the people he was responsible for...but he was for damn sure going to try.

The thought that had been on his mind since the crisis started came to the forefront of his consciousness, and he picked up his phone, cursing as the huge diesel generators supplying power to the post allowed the lights to dim and flicker. Hell, they would be using hand-powered crank phones next and bicycle to power the generators.

The General thought about the messages that had been flowing between Central Command, wherever the hell that was now located, and the posts in the Midwest. They used a lot of words to push a simple message. They were pretty much on their own. Triage, they called it. No resources for the middle of the country. So sorry. Do the best you can. Godspeed.

Christ, what a mess.

Snatching the phone from its cradle, he barked into the receiver, "Charlie, I need to talk to Sergeant McGill down in Springfield ASAP."

Hanging up the phone, he waited impatiently as his mind processed the information available. Could he fire on civilians? Even if it was a mob? If he gave the order, would his soldiers follow it? And, he knew he could legally fire on them, had permission to do so from the President, but would he? Would his people? The answer was easy. Yes. And for only one reason. To protect their family and friends.

He contemplated this for a few minutes until the phone rang. Snatching it from the cradle, he heard, "McGill on the line, sir."

"Seamus, you old reprobate. How's it hangin'?"

Sergeant Seamus McGill chuckled. "I'm doing as well as can be expected, General. Things are getting a little dicey here. I don't know how things are there, but here in Springfield, the folks are getting restless."

The General sobered immediately. Trust McGill to cut right to the chase. "I understand, Sergeant. It is the same here for everyone not on the base. Food is scarce. Good drinking water is hard to find since the pumps to the wells quit, and no fuel to take people out of here to the promised land, wherever the hell that is. Why shouldn't the natives be restless? We are already seeing movers fleeing St. Louis. That is why I reached out to you. I need to call in a favor."

"You don't need to call in anything, General. Just say the order. You know that."

"This is personal, Seamus. I need your help. You know my daughter lives in Springfield?"

"I'm aware of that, sir," McGill replied.

"Things are falling apart, Seamus. We both know that. It is going to be worse than anything in our experience in a short amount of time. Martial law has been declared by the President with no restrictions. We are ordered to keep the military viable at the expense of the populace. Do you know what that means? The Midwest is on its own."

"Well," Seamus said. "I don't like it much, but I do understand. What would you like me to do, sir?"

"Seamus, I need you to secure my daughter, Alice—same last name, never been married—and get her to Sanctuary on Lake Stockton. You have been there before. We have enough supplies stored there to last a good long while, and it is defendable. This needs to happen very quickly."

Seamus said seriously, "I assume when I go AWOL, you'll vouch for me?"

"Of course, I will, Sergeant. But, if things shake out like I expect, there won't be anyone to complain to. This is dead serious."

He continued briskly, "Now, I have to go, and you have work to do. Can I count on you?"

McGill cleared his throat. "You have my word, sir. Will you be joining us at Sanctuary?"

"If I can. Doubt it, though. I think we are going to get FUBAR'd, and we're going to get it in a big hurry. You watch your six. And, Sergeant?"

"Yes, General."

"I have ordered all our personnel and dependents into the Fort. There are just too many weapons and munitions here to give it up. You know what that means." The last was more of a statement than a question.

After a long pause, Seamus answered. "I understand, sir. It has been a rare privilege to serve with you. Join us if you can. Godspeed."

There was a catch in the General's voice only a good friend could hear. "Tell Alice I love her."

SERGEANT SEAMUS MCGILL sat at his desk, still holding the phone, as he stared out the window thinking of what he needed to do.

Few people knew of Sanctuary. The General was a rich man from old money, certainly not from his career in the Army. A few years ago, seeing the direction the country was heading, he had spent millions to build a safe house on Stockton Lake. He named it Sanctuary. It could not be seen from the air and was built into a bluff overlooking the lake. The only access was from the lake itself, except for one trail more suited to a mountain goat, and southwest Missouri didn't have a lot of those. The only way to assault Sanctuary would be by artillery from across the lake. Not a likely scenario. Or a flotilla of bass boats would work. It would be doable but costly.

The only sounds he could hear from outside the building were the roaring of diesel truck engines. They had procured huge snow movers from the highway department, the kind with the point on the front of the big blades that threw snow both directions, and were using them to clear some of the major streets of abandoned cars and trucks. He realized now that they were just wasting valuable fuel. If the General was right, and he was rarely wrong, none of this would help them, and by the time those in charge realized what was going on, it would be too late. He didn't have a whole lot of faith in the current crop of brass above him.

His problem, at least for now, was the same as the General's. The General could easily have hopped onto a chopper and come himself for his daughter. But, like Seamus, he could not just walk away from his unit. He could not shirk the responsibility; he was too old school for that. But he knew someone locally. If he could get this man to help, the General's daughter would be in good hands. First thing in the morning, he would go find him.

"Corporal Jennings!" he yelled through the door.

The sound of typing, or in this case, beating a keyboard into submission in the next room, never paused. He knew for a fact that she was working on her third replacement keyboard this month.

"Yes, Your Highness," came a shouted reply.

"Get me an address and location map for Mason Law. He lives here in town and should be in the special ops file."

"I'm on it, Your Grace."

Despite the seriousness of the situation, Seamus could not keep a smile from his face. "And put yourself on report for insubordination, Corporal. I'll sign it."

He heard a mixture between a snort and a snicker.

"Absolutely, sir. I'll see if I can find that particular form for you."

After the sound of a chair being pushed back hurriedly, Corporal Jennings poked her dishwater-blonde head, with the ever-present pencil stuck in her hair, around the doorframe.

"THE Mason Law?"

SEVEN

"ALICE. ALICE! WAKE UP." She felt someone nudge her feet and then kick her a little harder. "Rise and shine, bubblehead. They need you to come back to the ER."

Alice Slade groggily tried to look around. Hadn't she just left the emergency room? Of course, she had. So tired she could hardly stand, she had fallen asleep in a side corridor that led to the freight elevator with her back to the wall and knees drawn up to her chin. There were no lights showing because the hospital had been running on emergency generators, off and on, for two weeks and was rationing power. City power was just too unreliable.

She held up her hand to block the beam from the flashlight. "Who is that? Mary?"

"Well, who the hell else do you think it would be? Get your ass in gear, Alice. We gotta move. There's trouble."

Alice leaned her head back against the wall and closed her eyes. She had met Mary Chen in Afghanistan. Alice, since she was a general's daughter, had done her stint in the Army and more time in Afghanistan than she cared to remember. Mary was a nurse in a MASH unit and had talked Alice into learning a trade that didn't include, as Mary put it, blowing people away. Some days, she wondered if it was a good decision.

Coming back to the matter at hand, Alice said, "There is always trouble, Mary. That's why they call it an emergency room. Besides, I just left that damned zoo. It couldn't have been an hour ago. That place was wound tight as a baseball. Surely things haven't unraveled in that amount of time."

"Yeah, well...not to downplay your organizational skills, but you haven't looked outside lately. Your ball of twine is not lookin' so good and is unraveling at a high rate of speed."

Alice thought about that a moment. Even as she wondered why they needed her, she knew the answer. She was a good nurse, but she also knew she was at her best whipping things into shape and bringing order out of chaos. She was an organizer, a workhorse, and naturally bossy. At barely over five feet tall, and as the men commented, built in all the right places, she knew she could be a human dynamo when she needed to be.

When Alice still didn't move, Mary turned and put her back to the wall, then slid down to sit. Alice could barely see her in the dim light, but knew her friend was watching as she reached into the pocket of her nurse's smock and pulled out a pack of cigarettes. It was a habit she'd picked up in Afghanistan, where boredom and mind-numbing adrenaline were metered out in equal portions. With a sigh, she started looking for her lighter.

"Not in here, Alice," Mary said. They had a running,

good-natured argument about Alice's smoking habit. "Where do you find those things, anyway?"

Alice wistfully held the cigarette under her nose and smelled it. "The smoking police speak again. You really need a vice, Chen."

Alice continued as she reluctantly put away her pack of cigarettes. "You know, let's not go back. Hell, we aren't doing much good, anyway. Let's just fade out of here and go away. We're out of everything we need. Every bed is full. Most of the hallways are full. The waiting rooms are full. Half the doctors are gone, and a good part of the nurses. The cafeteria is short of food, and they are having a hard time feeding patients. If it gets any worse, I don't know what we will do. We need to grab our go-bags out of the locker and bug the hell out of here."

"Yeah, I know," Mary continued the conversation. "And, to sweeten the pot, I hear the generators have quit for good. They are done. Toast. We are officially in the dark, and when I left the ER, Dr. Turner was about to have a coronary. Which," Mary amended, "would be worth the price of admission. The little prick."

Alice chuckled as she lifted herself to her feet with a groan, stretched, and rolled her head around on her neck. Finally, she reached a hand to Mary and helped her up. "We'll do what we always do, Mary. We go to work and do what we can. We will even work with your favorite doctor."

"Wee Weenie Turner has been trying to get in my pants for months," Mary complained as she shortened her stride to keep pace with Alice, the beam of her flashlight bouncing around the walls.

"So, let him," Alice joked.

"What?" Mary snickered. "Even I have standards,

Alice. You know I'd like to marry a nice doctor, but the first standard is 'size does matter' and the second is 'thou shalt measure over...'"

Mary's voice faded as soon as they turned the final corner, and a full wave of sound, previously muted by the twists and turns of the corridors, hit them full in the face, and Alice could see at a glance the emergency room was coming apart at the seams. Any full emergency room is controlled chaos at best. But, right now, this one was approaching mayhem. And darkness made it worse.

The battery-powered emergency lights over the doors had long since given up. There had not been enough electricity to charge them. The only lighting came from the little penlights that almost every nurse and doctor carried. Thank God they still had a good supply of those. The room looked to be full of maddened fireflies.

One of the harried nurses was walking among all the people in the waiting room with a clipboard and flashlight, giving each a number. Or trying to. Most ignored her. The nurses had given up having patients come to the little cubicles for an interview. There simply was no room for privacy. Now, they could hardly see who was injured the worst. And they were all injured. There were no sniffles, sore throats, or belly aches out there.

As they walked by one of the trauma rooms, Dr. Turner hurried out. As soon as he saw Alice, he pulled her aside, turning his back on Mary, which evoked a very unladylike snort from her.

"Alice, we're in deep shit here. I want you to take over the ER. I'm way over my head." He ran his hand through his thinning hair and stared vacantly toward the waiting room. "Security says there is fighting in the streets, over food of all things. The injured just keep pouring in. I don't..."

She put her hand on his arm and interrupted. "Where is the D.O.N.? She should be here."

Dr. Turner laughed softly. "Her husband came and got our director of nurses an hour ago. He said it was too dangerous here." He looked directly at her. "Besides, I'd want you in charge anyway. Weren't you in the Guard or something? A battlefield nurse?"

"We were regular Army," Mary interjected. "Not the damned Guard."

Screaming erupted from the waiting room, and a nurse came running in, the light from her flashlight bouncing off the walls. "I cannot control it out there." She stood looking at them, frustration and fear showing on her face and in her voice. "I don't know what to do."

Alice took a deep breath and let it out slowly. How did the old saying go? The worst thing to fear in an emergency is...fear. Fear is contagious and has to be controlled. The second worst thing is indecision. She took a moment to remember everything she had ever learned about battlefield triage, gathered herself mentally, and then stood erect. She had not earned the title of Little General for nothing.

"Okay." Her voice carried through the noise. "How many doctors do we have left right now?"

"Myself and Bartholomew," Turner said.

"Here we go." Mary chortled. "The General's daughter. Front and center."

"Shut up, Mary." Alice smiled at her to take the sting away and then realized they really couldn't see much of each other anyway with no lights. Then she said, "Dr. Turner, as of this moment, we are in full triage, and I do mean full. You take trauma one and don't leave it. Tell Bartholomew to stay in trauma twelve, across the hall."

"But all the rooms are full," Turner interrupted.

"Then, clear them out! Grab any nurses that you need to work with you. From this moment forward, any patients you treat will be brought to you. If we don't bring them to you, ignore them. Don't go running around looking for something to do. When you run out of supplies, steal from the other trauma rooms. In fact, we need to assign someone to start robbing from everywhere right now."

Alice took a deep breath and started walking toward the waiting room. "Mary, I want you to round up the youngest aides and nurses, or for that matter, anybody you can find. Especially anyone you remember who has bragged about how much they run, how fast they are, or how good their condition is."

"Wha…?" Mary wondered aloud.

"Come on, Mary. Work with me. No power. Phones don't work. Radios don't work. The only communication we have is handwritten notes and verbal orders delivered by the 'ankle express' folks you are going to enlist. And be quick about it. I've got other things for you to do."

Dr. Turner interrupted. "What if I have to operate? We can't get to the operating room."

Alice had not stopped walking. "I said triage, Doctor, and you damned well know what that means. We save the people least injured first and turn them loose to make room for more. People with more serious injuries will be next. If anyone needs an operation today, they are SOL, and you will never see them. We have to let them go."

Dr. Bartholomew, a tall stooped-over figure that they always thought looked like a mix between Abe Lincoln and Count Dracula, stepped in front of her, followed by a couple of frazzled nurses.

When he spoke, his voice was deep and cavernous... and plaintive. "We can't do anything in here, regardless of triage. We can't see."

Mary grabbed him by the coat front and pulled him toward trauma twelve. "Think, people! Work with me." She looked over her shoulder. "Mary, are you still here?"

"Yes, General, ma'am."

"Grab a bunch of penlights or bigger flashlights if you can find them. There may be some battery-powered floodlights on the ambulances. Make bundles and tape them to an IV pole so poor Dr. Bartholomew can see." The last ended sarcastically, and the doctor grimaced.

"Earl!" Alice yelled into the darkness for the head of security. It was a rare day when he was not lurking around somewhere close, and they had become friends. "Earl! Where are you hiding?"

Earl Stokes was getting along in years but could still move when he needed to. He came bounding up from the darkness. "Here, Miss Alice."

She heard the crackle of static even as she asked the question. "Hey! Do your handhelds still work?"

"Yes, but only for a while, Miss. We don't have any way of charging them now."

Alice thought for a moment, staring at the milling people in the waiting room. "Earl, call as many security people or anyone else that you can. Get them down here and clear this waiting room. I want every patient concentrated in the ambulance bay. Don't take no for an answer. Just move them out of here. Use your gun if you have to."

"I don't have a gun, Miss Alice," Earl said apologetically.

Alice sighed and put her hand on the old man's shoulder. She knew his position here was mainly for show, but he was all they had. "Earl, you'd damn well better find one. You're going to need it."

Even as she responded to Earl, her other hand reached out and snagged one of the paramedics that tried to push by her. "Do we have any ambulances with enough gas left in them to run? Or any kind of vehicles, for that matter?"

"Uh..." the man stuttered a moment. "They'll run, but there isn't enough fuel to go anywhere very far. Besides, we are not going out anyway. It's way too nasty out there, and we could fill the gurneys just from the parking lot."

"Look," Alice said. "Here's what we need." She proceeded to tell the man and a few more who had wandered up, what she wanted. "Pull your vehicles as close together as possible with their lights shining into the ambulance bay. I want the vehicles tight together, practically door to door, except for just enough space for one line of people to get through from the outside, coming up to that door." She pointed at the door and then made a square with her hands. "Box it off. It will give us more security and some light to work with."

"What happens when we run out of gas?" one man from the small crowd that had gathered asked.

"Then we run on batteries. By the time the batteries run down, maybe it will be daylight. If not, we will rub sticks together and make a fire. Let's get cracking, people. We have work to do."

As Alice stood surveying the activity around her, she could see a semblance of order taking shape. People began moving with purpose again, grim determination showing on their faces. It was a start.

One of the nurses asked, "What about the people in the other rooms? What do we do with them? Shouldn't we give them our first priority?"

Now for the hard part.

Alice shrugged her shoulders, ignoring the twinges of guilt. "They have already been treated. If they are going to make it, they will. If not, we probably couldn't save them anyway. Not with what we have to work with now."

"But..." the nurse started to argue.

"Dammit! No buts." Alice grabbed the nurse and pointed her toward the ambulance bay. "There are people out there that are dying right now. They have been shot, stabbed, beat up, and broken. Go help them. If they need something that you or the doctors can't do right here, right now..."

God forgive her.

"...forget them. Have the orderlies take them outside and go to the next one."

Alice looked at the luminous dial on her watch. It was two a.m. Four hours to daylight. And what then? How would that change anything? She could hear sounds of fighting outside, gunshots and screaming, sounds of anger and pain. Who were they fighting? What were they fighting about? It could not be much different if they were back in Afghanistan and the perimeter had been breached.

Despairing, she looked around. The doctors had lights to work with, sort of. The small security force was ushering people out of the waiting room in some semblance of order. The vehicles were giving enough light the nurses could actually see what they were dealing with. She ran one hand through her short blonde hair, pulling it back from her forehead. *What else? What else?*

Mary came up beside her and put an arm around her waist. "I suppose you can have that cigarette now."

For the first time in hours, she smiled.

EIGHT

SOMEONE VIGOROUSLY TRYING to pound the paint off his door roused Mason out of a tortured sleep. He had spent the remainder of the night on the couch since he didn't want to face the bedroom again. There were too many memories in that room, not to mention Anne's reproving gaze from her picture.

He groggily thought of firing a round through the door. Maybe two rounds. About crotch-high.

"Law, you in there?" The pounding on the door began again.

Mason groaned as he thought he recognized the voice, got up, and walked toward the door. The way his back hurt, he would have been better off sleeping on the floor.

"Well, where the hell else would I be at..." he yelled as he glanced at a clock on the wall. "...six o'clock in the morning?"

He opened the door, took one look, and said, "Oh, shit!"

Sergeant Seamus McGill stood grinning at Mason. "Now is that any way to greet an old friend?"

Mason slowly stuck out his hand. "Depends on why the old friend is here. I can't think of any good reasons. Every time I see you, I get sent on long vacations to triple-canopy resorts full of very nasty people."

As they shook hands, Mason said, "So, what brings you to my humble home?"

"I need a favor, Mason. The favor is actually for General Slade. To be more accurate, he laid it on me to take care of, and I am now laying it on you. Remember the Major General? The one you were supposed to report to? Before you took a flyer out of that transport? He's up in Fort Wood right now."

"So what is the big favor?" Mason warily asked.

"As a favor to him, and to me, we need his daughter evacuated to the General's safe house by Stockton Lake, about forty miles from here as the crow flies. That should be a cakewalk for someone of your remarkable and renowned skills."

"Hire a crow."

"They are all booked up. Tourist season."

"You are serious, aren't you? Why me? Stick her in a Humvee and take her up there. You'll be back in four hours, tops."

"Mason, have you looked around you? We're falling apart here. There may not be anyone alive in this city in a week. The Army and whatever is left of law enforcement is going to have its hands full. I cannot leave my unit. Not now."

Mason thought for a moment. "I gave all that up, Seamus. You know that. I lost my edge when Anne died. I'm just not gung-ho for the cause anymore."

"So, be gung-ho about getting your ass out of town and take a good-looking woman with you. The last I saw her, she was cute as a button. That girl could die here, or worse. Have you looked around, Mason? Really looked? In a few days, this place is going to be like Somalia. I saw a little kid. Couldn't have been more than ten years old, walking down the street with a pistol in his hand. I don't know where he was going or what he was doing, and I didn't stop to ask."

McGill continued. "Someone has to make it out of this mess. We are asking, Mason. I'm asking."

"What about the guard unit here in town?" Mason asked.

"Can't be used. Can't be spared. Not going to happen."

Mason stood, looking off into the distance. Finally... "Dammit, Seamus. You don't play fair."

"I'm not playing. This is not a game. You owe me, Mason. Please. I'm asking."

Mason looked at the man he had known, off and on, for years. "Oh, alright. You know I'll do it. No need to get all squishy and maudlin. You had me from the handshake."

With a sigh of relief, Seamus gave Mason a map with the destination at Stockton Lake marked on it. "A few years ago, the General built a safe house up at Stockton. He calls it Sanctuary, and believe me, it is. It is a survivalist's dream; you just have to get there with your package in one piece."

Seamus handed him a picture of the woman. "Her name is Alice Slade. I'm acquainted with her, but I really don't know much about her except that she is the General's daughter and he wants her out of here. She is a nurse at Mercy Hospital and works in the ER. Short, about five feet tall, with blonde hair. She is ex-army and is feisty as hell. Runs with a gal named Mary Chen whom she met in the Army. Hell. This is the Midwest. There can't be more than a few hundred blonde nurses over there, so she should stick out like a sore thumb. Given all the gunfire I heard overnight, there should be lots of business at the hospital, and she should be easy to find."

"How much time do you think we have, Seamus? Before things crash."

Seamus looked at him steadily. "Less than none. We're in a death spiral right now. The Major General said to expect a FUBAR and didn't think he would make it out of Fort Wood. I concur with his assessment. You have a little time right now. Most mobs and crowds are quiet for a while in the mornings, so I would expedite and haul ass before they get cranked up again."

"Does she know I'm coming?" Mason asked.

"Do they ever?" Seamus replied with a laugh.

"Alright, I'll do what I can."

Hell, I got nothing better to do.

MASON HAD JUST CLOSED the front door when his back door started rattling. He started that way. *What the hell now?*

He snatched open the back door. "What!"

The Admiral tried to peek around Mason's shoulders. "Did you just have visitors?"

"Absolutely. That was just a chorus line of nude dancers leaving, plus the rest of the neighbors and some circus performers...what took you so long to get here?"

"Smart ass! I have breakfast going on my back porch, Law. We need to talk."

"Why so early?" Mason asked. "We were up half the night."

"And the day is half gone," the Admiral replied.

"Fine." Mason sighed. "Hell, I got nothing better to do. Wait. Actually I do have something to do. I'll need to leave pretty quickly."

"Roger that, but at least take time for breakfast. And start filling every container you have with water. That water tower will start going dry as soon as their backup generator and pump runs out of diesel."

The Admiral went stalking off, and Mason slammed the door so hard the windows rattled. He went to see the only container he was concerned about right now.

He was thrilled beyond reason the stool would still flush.

MASON FOUND the Admiral scrambling eggs and flipping sausage on his outdoor grill. With the flat pizza pan on top of the grill, he could use it just like a wood stove. The origin of the eggs was a mystery since he assumed the stores were empty, until he looked deeper into the backyard and saw a few chickens running around. He deposited himself on a high stool that bellied up to a round, glass table.

"Propane tanks empty, Admiral?" It looked like he was using charcoal briquettes over the burners.

"You still don't get it, do you? We ran out of propane a long time ago," the Admiral replied. "When we're out of charcoal, I'll have to use wood."

He watched him for a few minutes, glanced at his watch again, and then said, "What's up, Admiral? We gonna solve all the world's problems this morning? I really need to run an errand."

"No, not everyone's problems. Just mine, I hope," replied the Admiral. "I need your help."

In the light of day, the white-haired Admiral looked frail compared to the last time Mason had seen him. He knew the Admiral had been retired for a long time and was probably pushing seventy years old, maybe older.

"I owe you, Admiral," said Mason. "I owe you for a lot. For taking care of Anne when she was sick, for standing in for me. I can't ever repay that."

"I understood why you weren't here. So did Anne." Admiral Holloway gruffly cleared his throat. "Several hundred people died about the same time here in the city. They called it a rogue virus. It was a sudden thing, you know? One day she was okay. The next day, she had a cough that turned into a fever. She was gone in three days." He cleared his throat again. "I loved her like my own daughter. Probably saw more of her than my own."

Both men were lost in silence for a moment.

"Wait." Mason finally asked the obvious question. "You have a daughter?"

"Yes, I have a daughter," the Admiral replied irritably. "I had a wife, too, until she ran off with some biscuit shooter from a fancy restaurant. I guess he could bake better than I could...probably tossed her salad better. But that was long ago and far, far away."

Mason could not suppress a grin.

The Admiral continued. "My daughter is the problem. I have not seen her in several weeks. Actually, since we started having power problems, although the power going out will not bother her. She went off the grid a long time ago, so she may not know the power went down or the danger involved."

The Admiral went on to tell him how his daughter lived on a small vegetable-producing farm out toward Everton, northwest of Springfield. She grew organic produce to bring into town and sell at the farmers' markets. At least she did until gas got scarce.

"I've got to get out there and check on her. I don't think she understands what's coming."

"Do you understand?" Mason asked softly, his gaze boring into the Admiral. "Do you know what's coming?"

The change that came over Mason Law startled the Admiral. Gone were the easy camaraderie and the quick humor. He had suddenly become deadly serious. For the first time, Mason was showing him the soldier hiding behind the happy-go-lucky facade.

"I didn't retire an admiral by being a dummy, Law." He shoveled eggs and sausage on two plates. "Of course I know what is coming. There are those of us who have been warning people for years. I have even done the talk show circuit with the conservatives, blogged on the internet, talked to civic groups, basically talked to anyone who would listen."

"All of which accounts for…nothing," Mason said. "The philistines are among us, so to speak."

"True," admitted the Admiral. "Years ago, the Marxists gained control, and we didn't even know it. No matter if we elected a Democrat or Republican, we always got the same thing. A progressive. Take the hide off them, and they all look the same. The last few years, the environmentalists finally got their way and shut down about all production of oil, all mining of coal and oil shale. The BP disaster in the gulf, while never proven to be sabotage because they investigated themselves, didn't help matters much. The government cut back natural gas production, and, of course, no new nuclear power plants.

"But, the biggest problem, Law, is that we don't produce our own food anymore. There is not a single city in the United States of any size that can feed itself. We ship it in from other countries, just like our oil. Supposedly, it is cheaper that way."

The Admiral shook his head in frustration, stabbing around at his eggs, but could not seem to bring any to his mouth. "What a bunch of damn fools.

"Do you know how many pounds of food used to be distributed through Springfield each day?" the Admiral resumed.

"I'll bet you can tell me," Law replied sarcastically.

"Over a million pounds. Springfield is the hub for the trucking companies that deliver all across southwest Missouri. That is a lot of food, Law.

"Finally," the Admiral continued. "All our enemies in the oil-producing countries figured out that we'd actually been this stupid. They could not believe it at first, and kept looking for the catch. Finally, they just stopped shipping. Venezuela nationalized about a dozen of our oil platforms off their coast. All the oil rigs off our shores are owned by the Chinese and Russians. Now, we cannot start producing again in time to save ourselves. All the environmentalists could not come up with enough wind and solar power to make a difference. We are trying to play chess when someone else owns the board. Checkmate."

He pinned Mason with a hard stare. "Law, do you

know how much food is left in the stores when the trucking industry stops for lack of fuel? Which it has, by the way."

Mason thought for a moment, suddenly not so hungry. "A couple of weeks? A month, maybe?"

"Just three damn days." The Admiral stopped pretending he was going to eat a meal and pushed his plate away. "There lies Springfield right over there, with a hundred fifty thousand people, give or take. In southwest Missouri, there are over a million people. The stores are running out of food. I doubt any restaurants are still open. The Army will keep their food under guard. Those who have prepared for this will have enough food to last a few months, but the normal citizen might have a week's worth of food in the house. The average apartment dweller, I call them beehives, might have a day or two supply. They didn't need a supply of food, because they always ate out somewhere. Power is out, so there go the freezers. What happens now? What happens to all the people wandering around getting hungrier by the minute and wondering how this could possibly be happening?"

Mason smiled a mirthless smile as he thought for a moment. "I suppose some will sit tight and wait for the government to feed them. Probably more than you can imagine will do exactly that. A good portion will rob their neighbors, storm any supply houses they think will have edibles, and there are some huge warehouses in town, like that Convoy of Hope and Ozark Food Harvest. Then, when they find out those places are empty, they will turn toward the military base at the airport. The police will not be able to control them. Hell, the police will not have food either. The Army will repel the attack at the airport and then airlift everything out, provided they have any fuel left. I have studied the scenario, Admiral."

"And when they've all been hungry for a week, women and kids crying, husbands and fathers desperate to help them?" the Admiral asked with a haunted look in his eyes.

Mason replied, "They will hit the countryside like locusts, thinking farmers are hoarding food. They will spread like ripples in a pool, killing anything in their path to get food and water. The survivalists call them the walking dead. Ah." Mason grinned. "Which brings us full circle, back to your daughter? You're a devious man, Admiral."

"She does not understand and will try to feed and help everyone who comes her way. And when people find out she has food? Game over. Mason, if you have any travelin' gear, you had better get it. I have just enough gas to get us there, with a little luck."

Mason slid off his chair and headed for his house. *Well, hell. What else do I have to do?* He stopped suddenly. Actually...he did have something to do.

"Give me a couple of hours, Admiral. When I get back, we'll load up and go," Mason said. He looked toward Springfield and noted plumes of smoke from several fires.

"Second thought, better make it three hours."

"We? Who is we?" the Admiral replied.

NINE

SEAMUS MCGILL WALKED into the smoke-filled office that was top-heavy with brass and came to attention. He stood that way for over a minute before the colonel in charge of the detachment at the Springfield Armory noticed him.

"McGill," Colonel Kessler said. "I understand you went to visit someone early this morning."

Seamus felt a cold knot forming in his stomach. *What the hell?* "Yes, sir."

"Why?" the Colonel asked.

"It was a personal matter. Just visiting a good friend," Seamus answered. "I was not aware we were confined to the base, sir."

The Colonel tented his fingers in front of his face, holding his gaze on the sergeant. "I also understand you are friends with Major General Slade."

"That's correct. We have served together on several occasions, sir." *Where was this going?*

"You know? I could just take you out and shoot you, Sergeant. I wouldn't even have to fill out paperwork."

McGill cursed himself for having left his sidearm in his desk.

"However," the Colonel continued. "You are a valuable asset to me, so I am going to let this slide and explain something to you. I have orders to carry out. So do you. We are ordered to bring everyone into the city so we can better meet their needs. The orders from Central Command about controlling the populace are by 'any means necessary.' Are you following me so far?"

"I believe it is beginning to become clear, sir," McGill said.

"My methods will be unorthodox but effective. When everything shakes out, we should have control over a pretty big chunk of land and resources. We will be the power here when things return to normal, not city or state governments or even federal. Just us with our own little chunk of real estate. Those who stick with me will be rewarded. However, I don't believe General Slade would approve of these methods. I also believe if I have his daughter under my protection, so to speak, the General will be more than cooperative and stay out of my way. To that end, I have dispatched a squad to go pick her up."

McGill lost all pretense of being polite. "I wouldn't want to be in your shoes if you harm that girl, Colonel."

"Oh, she won't be harmed. She will be very well taken care of. At least as long as we are not interfered with by the General. We should have her in our hands today."

Seamus could not help but smile.

"You find that amusing?"

"They will fail, sir."

"Really? And why is that?"

McGill pinned Colonel Kessler with his gaze. "The

Major General." He stressed the General's rank. "Ordered me to evacuate his daughter. I contacted Mason Law to carry out that order. At this time, Mr. Law has no allegiance to anyone here and in particular, not the Army."

"Why contact this Mason Law?" the Colonel asked.

"Mason Law is a Shepherd, sir."

Colonel Kessler backed slowly until he could lean on his desk. "Shit. I don't like this. I don't like this at all. How good is he?"

McGill decided to be truthful in hopes of keeping the Colonel away from Mason. "He is very capable, and will not be called off."

"What does that mean?" Lieutenant Stark interjected. "What is a Shepherd? I have never heard that designation put on anyone."

McGill looked at the lieutenant a moment, and then when he received a nod from the Colonel, he replied, "A Shepherd is an individual that we send into a hostile environment to bring out people that are in danger and that we need to keep alive. Mason Law has a one hundred percent record of recovery."

"So, he's some kind of Rambo? A killing machine? A SEAL team member? Ranger? What?" Stark said sarcastically.

The sergeant shrugged. "No. Look," he continued, exasperated that he should have to explain this to a general officer. "It's Survival 101. If you go into enemy country like a lion, armed to the teeth and looking for a fight—you will find it and sooner or later get the shit kicked out of you. That is counterproductive. Better to go in as a rabbit. A Shepherd relies on stealth and absolutely does not want confrontation with anyone. In fact, he avoids it like the plague, because if someone knows where he is and what he is doing, then a Shepherd can't do his job."

Lieutenant Stark smiled. "So, this superhero is a rabbit?"

McGill looked at the lieutenant coldly. "On the other hand, if people get in his way or start shadowing him after an extraction...well, let's just say those folks disappear. No fanfare. No blaze of glory. Just...gone."

Colonel Kessler stood again and addressed the sergeant in a brisk tone. "Sergeant, according to our orders, we are tasked with bringing everyone into the city so they can be dealt with and controlled. That means everyone! You find this man, and you bring him in. The same rules apply to him as to everyone else. They come into the city, or we bury them. Period. Those orders are from the President. Do you understand?"

Killing civilians? "Begging your pardon, sir. It might be a better option to leave him alone. As I see it, the only harm he can do to us is if we piss him off. Better to just ignore him." He paused a moment. "And that includes the General's daughter. Besides," he added, "the General may never make it out of Fort Leonard Wood. But, if he does make it out and you have harmed his daughter? You will not survive that."

"Sergeant, you let me worry about the General. We have to have this area under tight control. I cannot tell you all the plans at this time, but we must control everyone. Civilian and military. Every last person within this sector. Do you understand that? We don't need someone running around that can bind people together or become some sort of loose cannon. We need to keep focused on the plan."

"Oh, I understand the orders, Colonel," McGill

replied. "It is the implementation that concerns me. Don't you realize that with summer coming on, there are farms and communities in the surrounding areas that can help feed these people? I can maybe see keeping the city folks here so they don't overrun the farms, but to round everyone up from the country and small outlying towns and bring them into Springfield is madness."

Lieutenant Stark spoke sharply. "That's enough, Sergeant. Don't forget who you are talking to."

McGill gave Lieutenant Stark a hard stare. "I am very aware of whom I am speaking to, Mr. Stark. Very aware."

Lieutenant Stark was starting to advance toward the sergeant when the Colonel interrupted.

"Alright, that is enough. You are dismissed, Sergeant. See to your duties," the Colonel said. "And don't, under any circumstances, leave this facility or try to warn your friend Mr. Law."

"I thought you just told me to find him?" McGill said tightly.

"That order is rescinded."

AFTER MCGILL LEFT, the Colonel said, "Lieutenant, I hope you know I just saved your life. The sergeant would chew you up and spit you out without raising a sweat. That's a fact."

"I doubt it, sir. I've been trained by the best. I have not been beaten in years. Do you think this Shepherd is as good as McGill says?"

"No one is that good, Mr. Stark. I have heard that he always gets the job done, regardless of the difficulties. We can only assume he is dangerous. These enlisted men always stick together, and I expect them to exaggerate their prowess. But we have to find a way to get the woman, and we may have to take care of Law in the process. I agree with McGill that once he has agreed to extract Miss Slade, he will not back off. There has to be a way. I expect you to take care of those details, Mr. Stark."

"You can count on me, sir."

After Lieutenant Stark left, the Colonel sat at his desk, staring blindly out the window. A side door opened, and a large man stepped inside. Dressed in boots, jeans, and tee shirt, he still looked like a military man.

"You heard?"

Kirk Wells nodded as he crossed the room to stand in front of the desk. "He won't be in time."

"We still need her," the Colonel said.

"I can get her," Kirk said. "Just remember our agreement."

"I remember. You will be right beside me when this all shakes out. All the power in the world. We'll live like kings."

KIRK WALKED OUTSIDE and strode toward another building to meet with some of his men. He might live like a king, but it wouldn't be here. He had been cozying up to the General's daughter for months. In an unguarded moment, Alice had told him about Sanctuary. When things had started falling apart, he remembered the conversation. Once he had control of that place, the new world would, indeed, be his for the taking. The change of plans was acceptable. Law would be successful. He would just meet her there.

And the Colonel?

Dead man walking.

WHEN SEAMUS MCGILL walked back into his office, he was steaming mad. At forty-eight years old, he had served his country for thirty years. But he didn't sign up for this. He knew the Army didn't have enough food for the civilians. The city would be a death trap for both civilians and military, just because of a military commander who wanted to be a king. With the number of people they were trying to shove into the town, disease would be rampant. Starvation and desperation would follow. After that, he knew that no amount of military control would hold the people in this city.

McGill pulled his handgun from the top right desk drawer, checked the load and safety, and placed it next to his hand on the top of the desk. In those few seconds, he mentally crossed a line he never imagined he would cross. There was no indecision. His path was clear.

Corporal Jennings walked in. As usual, she had read his mind and came in before he could call for her. When she noticed the gun on the desk, she quipped, "I swear to God, I didn't mean to put your age at a hundred on that fitness report, sir."

"Close the door, Gretchen," Seamus said quietly.

She stopped so quickly she skidded on the wooden floor. Her face reflected her surprise.

"Gretchen?" she said.

Seamus was sitting at his desk with his head in his hands. Then, with determination settling on his face, he looked at her.

"Gretchen, I trust you," he said.

"What's up, sir? Has something happened?"

Seamus watched her as she stiffened and then seemed to relax a fraction. "Telling me you trust me is about as bad as a spouse saying, 'we need to talk.' You aren't going to dump me for that redhead over in supply with the big tits, are you?"

He smiled as he said, "This is more about keeping you."

"Well, it is about time," she said. "After all, I've had your back for the last five years."

Seamus was well aware of her abilities and of her feelings for him. That he had never responded was more of a sense of duty and not fraternizing with those under his control than any dislike for her. Actually, he had wanted her for a long time.

"Are you aware of what is going on in the city and the country?" he asked her.

She sighed. "I got eyes, Seamus. It doesn't take a crystal ball to tell the fortune of this country, or of this community."

He was still putting his thoughts together, even as he spoke. "Gretchen, we both swore an oath to protect this country from all enemies, foreign and domestic."

"Yeah, and to obey lawful orders from a superior officer. How's that workin' out for you?"

She had been moving slowly toward him until she came around the desk and stood next to him. Nudging him with her hip, she said, "C'mon, Seamus. You are starting to scare me. Spill it."

He told her everything that was going on and what he believed the future held for their unit. When he got to the part about controlling the civilians, her gasping intake of breath was enough to tell him her opinion of that.

"Gretchen, do you have family in town? Anyone?" He looked up at her expectantly but was surprised by her quick response.

As she answered him, she pulled her sidearm, identical to McGill's, racked the slide and chambered a round. He saw her thumb up the safety as she returned the gun to its holster.

"All my relatives are back east. And if you're asking, no romantic ties here. If you had half a brain, you would know that, and why. Sir."

Seamus glanced toward the closed door. "Look, this is personal, so I can't order you. I can only ask. Gretchen, I'm going to go on a hike. I am going to bug out of here before it is too late. There is simply nothing we can do here. Maybe we can go up around Stockton Lake where General Slade's safe house is. It's a long walk, but vehicles are out of the question unless I can steal one out away from the city. It is going to be tough and dangerous. Actually, I am not sure we will even make it out of town."

He looked at her a moment, unable to continue.

She leaned against him, rubbing his back and shoulders. "So, will you ask already? A girl likes to be asked, Seamus."

"Alright," he said. "Will you go with me, Gretchen?"

"Yes," she said briskly. "When do we leave?"

"Just as soon as we can gather some gear. We can't take too much, or anyone seeing us will be suspicious."

"How are we going to get away, Seamus?" She was already striding toward a locker in the room and pulling out a canvas bag.

"I think we need to inspect the perimeter around Springfield. Like the northwest side."

"Out by the airport? There is a detachment there." They both knew the helicopter repair facility was there along with the remnants of a rapid response unit.

"It is also the most open and the hardest perimeter to defend," Seamus said. "I don't think the town is sealed off yet, but we can't waste too much time."

She started toward the door when his voice stopped her. "There is one other thing. I'm going to give you the last order I ever will."

"And that is?" she said with a smile.

"Don't ever call me sir again."

"Yes, Your Highness."

THEIR OFFICES WERE at the old National Guard armory on the north side of Springfield. The grounds were fenced in, but with the madhouse of vehicles and soldiers constantly on the move, it was a simple matter to walk away. Both wore backpacks, utility belts with sidearms, and an M-4 on a sling down their backs. Every available pocket was filled with either ammunition or PowerBars for food. They didn't have much room for water, but had plenty of water purification tablets.

They had not gone far when they realized it would be hard to blend in with the crowd. Because of their uniforms, everyone they met gave them a wide berth.

"Gretchen, we need to change into 'civvies' as soon as we can. This is not going to work."

"What about the M-4s?" she asked.

Seamus thought about it as they walked. "We can

break them down and put them in our packs. If that does not work, we may have to ditch them."

The problem solved itself in the short term as they reached the edge of town. When they got to Kearny and Kansas Expressway, or Highway 13 North, they heard heavy machine gun fire from over by the Interstate. At this intersection, and closer to them, there was a squad of soldiers at the backs of two trailer trucks sitting in an open parking lot.

When Seamus and Gretchen walked up, Seamus asked, "What is going on over there by the Interstate, Corporal?"

The man he spoke to replied, "Crowd control, Sergeant. A few people are still trying to leave town by vehicle. We've been ordered to stop that."

Seamus digested that for a moment. "So, what is going on here with all these people?"

"We're trading food for guns, Sergeant. These MREs are an ugly meal, but I guess when you're hungry, anything is good."

The couple looked at the long line of people stretched out for blocks. Men, women, and children. Most had firearms, some didn't.

"What about the ones that don't have anything to trade?" Gretchen asked.

The Corporal looked at them with sad eyes. "They are SOL, folks. No guns, no food."

"Does the Colonel know about this?" Seamus asked.

"Who do you think ordered it? I believe the order is 'by any means necessary,' Sergeant. That is exactly what we are doing." He looked at Gretchen, then lowered his eyes. "When the women get hungry enough, they'll be trading other things. It's a buyer's market out here."

As if to make the point, they saw a young woman with two children talking to a soldier next to one of the trucks. As they watched, she had the kids sit down while she went into the trailer with the man.

Seamus pushed his way up to the Corporal with Gretchen trying to restrain him. "Corporal, you will release this food to the people with no strings attached. Is that understood?"

"Aw, c'mon, Sarge..."

"No strings," Seamus yelled at him as Gretchen pulled him away.

"Hey!" the Corporal replied hotly. "Don't be yelling at me! I could detain you, Sarge. The word is already out to bring you back."

With his hand on his sidearm, Seamus said, "You haven't seen us, Corporal."

The man just waved his hand. "Aw, get out of here. Hell, I'm of half a mind to do the same thing. Besides, we have been ordered to prevent vehicles from leaving. Nothing was said about people on foot. Need some MREs?"

Warily, Seamus looked at him, at several of the squad watching them, and then around at the trailers. "No, we're good. And Corporal? If you decide to bug out, take that lady with her two kids with you. She deserves better than what she's getting in that trailer.

"One other thing, Corporal. Do you have diesel in those tractors?"

"Yeah. So?"

"Just a little something you should think about," Seamus said. "If you and one of those trailers of food were to find yourselves up around Stockton Lake, you could about write your own ticket. You would definitely have a hot commodity. You would even have room to take a few people with you."

"Aw, the roads are blocked anyway. And there is no way I'd get past the guards at the intersection."

Seamus looked at him and said, "Improvise. Adapt. Use a diversion. I'm betting the road going north isn't blocked, just the Interstate going east and west. Think about it."

Gretchen started pulling him away and toward the shopping center.

"I thought you didn't want to draw attention to ourselves?" she asked, giving his arm a little shake. "This is why we are leaving, Seamus. It won't get better. Not for any of them. And certainly not for us if we stay."

"Yeah, you are right. It just pisses me off to see good soldiers acting like that. The Corporal seemed alright. Maybe he'll take a few with him."

"Soldiers are just people, Seamus. Colonel Kessler thinks he is in charge, but he is not. His little world and big plans are all falling apart. He just does not know it yet. There are no rules now. A man or woman can be as good or bad as they have the strength to be. It has always been that way."

Seamus stopped and looked at her. "Now, that was profound. You have quite a head on your shoulders."

Gretchen shook her head. "Not really. I'm just a girl that wants to avoid having to go into one of those trailers." She motioned to the ransacked and trashed strip mall in front of them. "Now, I'm thinking those stores have back doors, and after that is a whole lot of green space. Let's go for a walk."

Just as they got to the buildings, they heard one of the trucks start up behind them. It slowly pulled forward and started moving through the connecting parking lots toward the Interstate. The remaining truck and trailer were surrounded by the squad of soldiers.

The long line of civilians coming to trade their guns for food, whether by their own thoughts or someone's suggestion, suddenly decided to just take the food. After all, they had guns. There were hundreds of them and only a few soldiers.

Once the firefight started, the armored vehicle pulled away from guarding the Interstate exchange and raced to the aid of the soldiers guarding the food truck.

Instantly, people on foot and a few cars started streaming across the overpass going north. Nestled in with them was a tractor-trailer full of food.

"Well, would you look at that?" Seamus said. "That is a nice diversion. No one will be looking at us."

Gretchen just shook her head. "You are one devious man."

As they strode toward the buildings, Seamus thought of the task he had given Mason Law. He felt guilty because he should have done it himself, and would have, except for what he now believed was misguided loyalty. Deep down, he hoped Mason had ignored him. Deep down, he hoped Mason had cut and run.

TEN

MASON LEFT the Admiral's house and the subdivision and then turned south toward Springfield. When he came to the I-44 interchange, he was surprised to see the Interstate completely jammed with cars. When he had seen it the day before, it was crowded but still moving. People were milling around outside their vehicles, wondering what to do, while others were standing on top of their cars trying to see how bad the jam was. With what he had seen from the height of the overpass, he could have told them that the line of cars stretched as far as he could see to the west. Traffic coming into town was moving slowly, while outbound traffic was completely jammed. He found it hard to believe that people were using the last of their carefully hoarded gasoline to make it into the city.

Strange.

He heard a whistle and looked up to see a soldier working as a traffic cop, a soldier in full gear and armed—guess he wanted Mason to get off the bridge.

It was slow going with the traffic coming off the Interstate trying to merge with people coming in from the north. Then Mason noticed an armored vehicle blocking traffic that was trying to leave the city. As he watched, a driver tried to sneak around the mini-blockade, nearly ramming Mason's pickup. As the car went past, he saw frightened faces looking out of the passenger window; the back seat had kids and a baby seat. He flinched as he heard, more than saw, the results of their maneuver as a soldier began firing at the car from the armored vehicle and heard the screaming of onlookers and glass flying from the car. Looking in his rearview mirror, he saw the car with punched-in windows and pock marks from the bullets as it drifted to the right and went off the road. That effectively stopped any other attempts to bypass the roadblock.

Mason wiped his sweaty hands on his jeans and repressed the urge to go back and take out that machine gunner. He was sick at the thought of those kids. American soldiers firing on civilians? This was crazy. What the hell was going on?

He snapped his gaze forward in time to avoid another collision, and then the road opened up into four lanes going south. It looked like no one was being allowed to leave the city. Traffic was heavy, but not bumper to bumper. Looking at both sides of Kansas Expressway, he could see most of the shops and restaurants had windows broken, with looters still going in and out. He guessed the doors were too small.

As he passed through the Kearny and Kansas intersection, he heard firing behind him. This time it sounded like a small war.

What the hell was he doing? The General should have

sent a bunch of Angry Bird Air Cavalry down to rescue his daughter. This was madness.

Nearly every major intersection was jammed with traffic and soldiers. Traffic lights were not working, and no one seemed to know the four-way-stop concept. But that was a concept foreign to a lot of people. As he passed through the residential sections, he noticed a lot of people just walking around like they had nowhere to go and nothing to do. In his mind, he was screaming at them to go home and get off the streets.

When he finally got to Sunshine Street, he realized that across the road to the southwest was the federal prison. The grounds and parking lots of the prison were jammed with people. Seeing the number of orange jumpsuits in the crowd, he assumed the doors had been opened. *Swell.* Mason turned east and headed toward St. John's Mercy Hospital. At about two blocks from the hospital, traffic came to a standstill. It was just as well because, at that point, his beloved Dodge Ram ran out of gas, and he drifted to a stop. It was when he exited the truck that he heard the sounds coming from the direction of the hospital. He could hear gunfire and screaming and could see smoke starting to rise from the north side.

He grabbed his pack and fell in with a group of men heading toward the hospital.

"What's going on at the hospital?" he asked one of the men.

"We heard the hospital has been hoarding food. They got no right to do that, so we're going to see about getting some. We have families at home that need that food."

Cursing under his breath, Mason started running.

ALICE PAUSED JUST inside the south entrance to St. John's Mercy Hospital and stretched hard, arching her back, trying to ease the pain of too many hours on her feet. She could not tell if the sound she heard was the elastic in her sports bra popping or her back breaking. But, as bad as it was, her backache was insignificant compared to her feet. That is what hurt the most. She straightened and wiggled her toes, pretending there was a little feeling coming back down there, but so far, it was a fantasy.

She stood a while, waiting for Mary to catch up. Mary always had something to do or someone to talk to.

Last night had been a nightmare, and the morning hours had been brutal. Just about daylight, the injured had stopped coming in. Of course, there were plenty of injured people on the streets of the city; they just didn't have any way to get to the hospital. Crazy stories had come in about firefighters and police under siege, treating their own injured in the fire and police stations, barricaded against the hordes of people. Why firefighters were included in that report, she had no idea. But, she guessed, people were mad at anyone in authority.

One man was telling that the university auxiliary police station actually stacked bodies to use as a barricade. Bodies! This was the lower Midwest where civility was the norm and people actually stopped to help each other in times of need. Out in the country, people still picked up hitchhikers, for crying out loud. Stacked bodies? The world was going crazy. She hoped that in the daylight, things would settle down.

"Lookin' in fine form, Miss Alice." Earl, the security guard, stood grinning at her as she settled back into a normal posture and pulled down the tail of her stained smock that had ridden up way too high for prying eyes during the stretch.

"Earl, you should be sleeping somewhere, and you're way too old to be looking at the girls," Alice said with mock severity.

She had looked in the mirror often enough to know what he saw. Her blonde hair was done up in a functional ponytail for now. Her parents had blessed her with genes that left her looking fit, whether she was or not. Just a little tall for it, she could still pass for a gymnast. But trips to the gym were more for fun than fitness, and she was sure 'the girls,' as she called them, were jutting proud when she stretched.

Earl let loose with something between a cackle and a snort. "Never goin' to be that old, Miss Alice. Never at all. Besides, you'd raise the dead if you stretch like that again."

"Really." Alice looked at Earl and replied sarcastically, "I'll keep that in mind for the next Code Blue." Her tone turned serious. "Not to change the subject, Earl, but have you heard anything about getting the generators going again? We have every bed full in this hospital and no power. We're running out of options."

Earl instantly sobered. "I don't think the power is coming back. I know for a fact the power company has shut down for good, and I seriously doubt we will be getting any diesel for the generators here. We got a promise of a tanker truck from the army at Fort Leonard Wood, but I doubt we will get it. I'd bet they got problems of their own."

"What about the guard units at the airport? Surely they have fuel." She knew the National Guard had taken over an old terminal building at the airport a year before and brought in a rapid response unit for deployment against terrorism.

Earl shook his head. "Nah. That's mostly aviation gas. What diesel they have will be for their own trucks. The last I heard, the whole unit was deployed to control rioting in St. Louis."

"But this is a hospital. We should have priority," she argued.

Earl held his hands up in mock surrender. "I'm just sayin' how it is. Don't get your dander up."

Alice thought of all the patients that would die if circumstances didn't change, mostly the old and people with chronic diseases like diabetes. Without insulin, those folks were gone. Well, maybe it would be a blessing. Some patients would be better off dying now rather than being released from the hospital to starve, and if last night were any indication, there might not be anyone to take care of them anyway. If not for the hospital food, she wouldn't have had much to eat, either. She knew whole families had packed into rooms, just hoping for some food. The cupboard was bare in their homes. And food supplies were scarce in the hospital. In a land that had so much of everything, people were running out of options and could not understand why.

She was not easily frightened. Already an army brat, she signed up at an early age, right out of high school. Her father, 'The General' didn't like that much, but she didn't care. She had no intention of following in her father's footsteps and making it a career. In training, they soon discovered that, no matter how far away they moved the target, she had a knack for putting a chunk of lead in it. Alice Slade became a sniper and was good at it. Her job was to take out the bad guys, and she did it well.

She had met Mary Chen when her spotter was killed, and Alice had taken a glancing blow to her helmet. They had brought her in unconscious and she spent a few days getting her feet under her.

Instantly becoming a good friend, Mary had convinced her it was time to stop being a target and do some good in life, so Alice had taken accelerated training and became a nurse.

She would only admit it to herself, but a certain callousness came along with the training she had. When she considered the breakdown in the community observed over the last two weeks, she was admittedly afraid. Everything was coming apart. Communication was spotty to nonexistent. The city had maintained power, although rationed, until last night, and then that had stopped. Generators were useless. A patrolman had told her that, even if someone had hoarded fuel for their generator, as soon as it was started, someone would show up and steal it and the fuel. Usually with disastrous results for the owner.

Alice thought back to her days in the Army. The circumstances around her were like watching a medivac chopper with its tail rotor shot off, winding out of control, pilots fighting the inevitable, and finally gravity taking over with the sudden stop and loud noise at the end.

The sick and injured just kept pouring into the hospital, demanding care. Demanding food and water. Demanding what no one had to give. Demanding. Angry.

The last ambulance they had sent out had not come back, and the rest of the crews wouldn't go. There were armed guards at the pharmacy down the hall, and from the looks of them, they might be guarding the drugs for themselves. Christ, what a mess.

As she gazed out the door at the sea of people, Mary Chen finally came hustling up. It was time to go.

Mary and Alice shared an apartment just a short walk from the hospital, or they wouldn't think of leaving now, even though the shift was over. Shift? Everyone was working until they dropped from exhaustion. The only way to get rest was to leave the building. And they both were bone tired. She and Mary had discussed leaving and thought if they could just get home and sleep about twelve hours, then they could re-group.

"Hey, Mary," Alice greeted her friend. "Earl says all I have to do to revive a code patient is this. What do you think?"

Alice raised her hands above her head again and shook top to bottom.

Mary replied, "Oh, stop it."

COMING into the parking lot at St. John's Mercy from the west, Mason had no idea where the emergency room was located, so he opted for the front entrance. All he could see was chaos. It seemed every foot of space in the lot was covered with vehicles or people. Somehow, the mass hysteria that was taking place—and hysteria was the only way he could describe it—had affected people's ability to park their vehicles in the spaces between the lines in the parking lot. Cars and trucks were parked haphazardly wherever they had stopped or run out of gas. The spaces between the vehicles were filled with people, all facing toward the hospital. The only movement was slow and sluggish toward the hospital. There didn't seem to be much conversation between anyone. It seemed to him that everyone was waiting for something to happen.

Mason pushed, shoved, dodged, cajoled, and threatened his way to the front of the crowd that was stopped about a hundred feet from the front door. The people reminded him of lemmings about to go over a cliff. The ones at the front were stopped and digging in their heels, but the sheer weight of numbers pushing from the back kept moving them forward.

As he made it to the front of the crowd, he saw a group of nurses come out the front doors and stop. Seeing a tall Asian nurse and wondering just how many of those there could be, he hoped one of the other nurses was Alice Slade. Pulling the photo from his pocket that Seamus had given him, he compared it to the short blonde's face and wished there was someplace he could buy a Lotto ticket. It was his lucky day. He rode the front of the wave of people moving inexorably toward the hospital.

ALICE FOLLOWED Mary Chen and the herd of multi-colored uniforms as they walked out of the south door of the hospital into the mid-morning sunlight. She knew they didn't have another ounce of energy left after the nightmare last night. *Bedraggled and draggin' our asses.*

A flick of her lighter and she started an inhalation that lasted an impossible amount of time.

Without looking back at her, Mary asked, "Alice, when are you going to give that up?"

"Bite me, Chen," Alice said with a smile. "I haven't had a good cough in twenty-four hours. I deserve this."

Alice started to follow up with another caustic remark when the group of nurses in front of her suddenly stopped, and her brain finally registered what was going on around them.

"Whoa, girls."

She spread her arms as wide as her five-foot frame would let her. In front of them was the parking lot, an area crowded with people just standing around, shoulder to shoulder, or sitting on cars. The crowd stretched as far as she could see. The strangest thing was the sound. It was like a low-level hum filled with countless voices, running footsteps, and stifled screams that all came as one moaning noise from the surrounding people.

And there were thousands of people.

"Why are all these people still here?" Mary asked her.

Since the emergency room was on the other side of the building, and while barricaded by the ambulances that blocked the view, those inside could not see the masses of people congregating outside.

"They have been here since the power went out. I thought they would have left last night, but the crowd has grown bigger," Alice said. "If you'd come out of your hole once in a while, you'd know this. Some are just lookin' for food, I guess. Some of them want to score some drugs. Some are hurt, but after last night, we can't take them in."

"Has anyone gone out and checked on the injured?" Mary asked.

Alice sucked in another lungful before she responded,

"You have got to be kidding me, Mary. Sometimes I don't think you're from this world. Have you looked real close out there? I don't think that is a very nice crowd."

As the nurses stood uncertainly on the sidewalk, Alice made an instant decision. There was no way they could get safely through that mass of people. She took Mary by the arm and started slowly backing toward the door. Alice took one final drag on her smoke and then flipped it toward the sidewalk. The crowd, almost as if by common consent, had begun moving toward the doors. Where before the hospital had once been considered a place of refuge, sacrosanct against violence, it was now simply a place that had things that people wanted or needed. And they were coming for it.

The low rumble of noise from the crowd was starting to grow.

"Girls, let's get back inside. Now."

When they didn't move quickly enough, she started shoving and yelling. "Now! Go!"

The startled nurses scrambled back toward the glass doors and scampered inside. As Alice glanced over her shoulder, she saw one of the nurses trying to run through the crowd. The wall of people stopped her. She saw the woman's despairing look back toward the hospital and a shriek of pain as countless hands tore at her. She went down with a gut-wrenching scream. The sea of people that surged forward were faceless and anonymous, except for one man carrying a military-looking rucksack over his shoulder that seemed to stand out. He was staring right at her.

Alice yelled at the security guard standing by the front desk. "Lock it down, Earl! Lock it down now."

Too late, the security man saw the danger and

reacted, rushing toward the door, fumbling for keys. But people were already pouring in and holding the doors open.

She glanced around, saw people crowded in all the corridors, and knew this was not the only door that the mob had stormed. Stormed? It was more like a coordinated attack against a defenseless position. *Jesus, would this day never end?*

Looking around at the mass of people, she saw the man with the bag over his shoulder still staring at them. Only at them, and starting to come toward them. *Strange.* But there really was not a choice on where to go or what to do and not a chance in hell she was going to ask him what he wanted.

"Up the stairs! Hurry, girls."

As she herded Mary and the small contingent of nurses toward the stairwell, she saw Earl go down under the wave of people. They simply knocked him down and then mindlessly stepped on him as they went by. She lost sight of him as she slipped into the stairwell and started running up the stairs. Behind her, there were gunshots and screams of anger. *There goes the pharmacy.*

Running up the stairs, she tried to think of some way to bar the doors shut, but there was no time. She didn't know what they would find at the top, but it had to be better than the bottom. With every step, she wondered if they should stop. It was just a crowd of people. Maybe they would run on by them if the nurses didn't resist. Maybe the nurses could mingle with the mob and be safe. Maybe...the screams and sounds of fighting coming from below them in the stairwell negated all of those thoughts.

They came out on the top floor and found a few

doctors and nurses staring at them with shocked expressions from the crowded, dim hallways.

Alice bent over for a moment, holding her side and gasping for breath.

"How do you like those smokes, now?" Mary asked her.

"If I could breathe, I'd slap you silly," Alice panted. "Should we try and bar these doors?"

Mary looked around her at the frightened people. "I don't think we can."

Alice could hear scrambling footsteps in the stairwell. *No time.*

"Hey, are you still friends with that medevac pilot?"

"If you call whenever he's horny as being friends," Mary replied.

"Well, let's go find him. And you'd better hope he's horny as hell because I don't see any other way off this island. We have to get out of here, and quickly."

"The last time I talked to him, they were really low on fuel," Mary said. "Although I'll admit, we didn't talk all that much."

Alice said, "We sure as hell need to get off this building. I don't see doing a last stand on the roof of this place. All I have for weapons are a couple of hemostats and a stethoscope."

A few people had stopped and tried blocking the stairwell door. Alice heard the door burst open with such force it slammed on its hinges against the wall and scattered the nurses. Suddenly a fusillade of shots sounding incredibly loud erupted from the stairwell, and the screaming started even louder behind them as they pushed through the doors onto the noisy helicopter pad. So much for a gun-free zone.

Alice turned at the doors and looked back. The man she had seen staring at them was at the top of the stairs, holding the door open and pointing a gun into the stairwell. She saw him fire into the stairwell. *God.*

It made no sense. Why were people hurting innocents? She had heard of mass hysteria but had never believed in it. Until now. As more gunshots erupted behind her, she turned and ran.

MASON FOLLOWED the nurses into the stairwell and fought his way upward. He could not believe his incredible luck in finding them in this melee of people. If they had not decided to come out of the hospital when they did, he would have never found them. People kept coming in from the floors they passed on their way up, and he kept pulling them down and shoving his way forward and upward. When he had gained a few steps on the people behind him, he pulled his .45 and fired a couple of rounds into the concrete steps. The people in front, hit by chipped concrete, tried to stop but were shoved forward by the mass of the people coming from behind.

When he got to the top, there were people on the other side of the door trying to hold it closed. It was not latched, and anger and adrenaline allowed him to kick it open. Everyone on the floor scattered as he turned and fired more rounds into the stairwell floor and then slammed the door so it would latch. That wouldn't buy him much time, but maybe enough. He turned as he heard the sound of a helicopter turning up the power and raced toward the landing pad.

ELEVEN

THE PILOT WAS JUST RUNNING up the rotors of the medevac chopper to full power when Alice and Mary slammed through the glass doors leading to the landing pad. His grim face broke a slight smile when he saw them, but he motioned them away. Ducking needlessly under the blades, they ignored him and ran to the open side door, crowding into the helicopter.

"Sorry," the pilot shouted over the high-pitched whine of the jet engine. "But you women will have to get off. I'm waiting for the administrator and some suits to evacuate."

Alice took one look back at the entrance doors to the helipad, crowded with fighting people. Pointing to the mass of people, she shouted, "I think they are going to exceed your load limit if you don't get moving."

She was startled when the emergency door next to the pilot was jerked off the aircraft, then a long arm entered, popped the shoulder harness release from the pilot, and unceremoniously ejected him from the pilot's seat.

As the pilot sprawled on the deck, the same man she had seen staring at them leaped in, threw his bag into the back, and yelled, "You had better strap in, ladies. We are going to dust out of here."

Only two things kept Alice in that aircraft. The first was the onrush of people trying to get out the doors and onto the helicopter pad. She knew there was no going back. The second was the new pilot's use of the word 'dust.' They barely had time to secure the side door when the new pilot lifted them from the deck under full power, and the collective pulled high. The helicopter seemed to leap from the pad like from a springboard. With the full-power drive into the sky, Alice knew instantly that the pilot was ex-military and felt a little more confident. He had obviously dusted off a few Landing Zones in his career.

The force of the takeoff pressed them down to the floor. A few seconds later, a half second of weightlessness signaled the G-force had let up, and their stomachs settled to their rightful location, except for one of the other nurses that threw up from the roller coaster ride. The pilot dropped the nose of the helo and settled into forward flight. Alice scrambled up and looked out the windows.

"Jesus God," she said, looking at the ground below. "Mary, look at that."

Surrounding the hospital parking lot was a mass of people running in and out of stores and houses, and bodies lying in the street. Buildings were burning in outlying neighborhoods, and one side of the hospital was on fire. As she watched, more explosions rocked the building.

"What?" Mary asked as she got to her feet, holding her stomach. She looked outside. "Sweet Jesus."

"Sounds like a prayer meeting going on back there,"

the pilot shouted above the sound of the wind whistling in through the missing door.

Alice forced her eyes from the ruin below her and shouted back. "Who in the hell are you?"

The pilot turned and grinned at her. "Please tell me you are Alice Slade?"

"What happens if I say no?" she asked warily.

"My name is Mason Law, and to answer your question, nothing bad. I'll just have to go back into that hospital and look for her."

Alice looked at him a moment and then came to a decision. "You got it right the first time. How do you know me? Why are you looking for me?"

"Your father called in some favors."

Alice said, "I think I have heard my father speak of you. Did my mighty father, the Major General, say if he would be joining us?"

Mason turned and looked at her a moment, made eye contact, then turned back to flying the aircraft.

She stared at the back of his head a moment. His glance at her had told the story, at least for her. All she needed now were the details.

"So, what's the story?" she asked.

Mason replied. "You're ex-military? You've seen action?"

"Mary and I were nurses in the Army, and yes, we have been in a few war zones," she said. "A lifetime ago."

"Look," Mason said. "I didn't talk to him directly. Seamus McGill relayed the request for your extraction from him. Seamus said your father was under siege by hordes of people from the St. Louis area. He was pulling back to protect the munitions and weapons."

He glanced at her again. "I'm sure you realize what that means?"

She nodded. Hordes of people. *Last stand at the Alamo.*

Alice flinched as, a moment later, a long-forgotten ripping sound entered her senses, felt more than heard, and one of the nurses gave a gurgling scream. She turned to find a nurse down and showered in blood, while Mary immediately dropped to her knees and tried to stop the bleeding. One glance told her it was useless. The round had come in through the bottom of the aircraft, took the obvious route through her body, and out the side of the nurse's neck. She never had a chance.

Alice whirled back and screamed at Mason. "We're taking rounds! They're right under us."

Mason immediately banked the aircraft to the right and dropped altitude to gain airspeed, then suddenly nosed up on a roller coaster ride that left them a good thousand feet higher and climbing. Only a spent round could hit them that high and wouldn't be likely to penetrate the hull.

When he had leveled out, Mason shouted back at them, "Sorry, ladies. I am not in 'war zone' mode yet. I should have had my head on a swivel. I didn't see that coming."

Mary came back to crouch next to her, and at Alice's questioning glance, shook her head. She stared at her bloody hands and leaned her head on Alice's shoulder as she silently cried.

Abruptly lifting her head off Alice's shoulder, Mary said, "I smell fuel."

"Sweet Jesus," Alice yelled back. "This is worse than the ER. It's one thing after another."

She turned and looked over the pilot's shoulder.

"Check your fuel gauge," she yelled into the incoming wind that was pouring in through the missing door. "I think we took a hit in the fuel cell." She watched as he leaned forward and tapped a dial on the instrument panel.

"Hard to tell. I don't think we started with much," he said. "We don't have far to go. Just a couple of minutes."

"Do you need someone in the other seat? I've done some stick time," Alice said.

"No, but I would really like some help getting strapped in. I'm about to blow out of here."

MASON WAS ENJOYING Alice leaning over him, trying to attach the safety harness. Her face was inches from his when she met his gaze. He smiled.

"Don't even think about it," she said.

His witty comeback died on his lips as the aircraft gave a couple of lurches, and the roar of the jet engine abruptly stopped. The only sound they heard then was the whine of the gearbox and the universal pilot's lament of, "Oh, shit!" as Mason quickly shoved Alice aside and disengaged the engine, stood on the rudder, and lowered the nose, starting what he prayed would be a successful autorotation. The helicopter started its death spiral as Mason began using the lift and energy from the rotors to keep control of the aircraft.

Mason's face was grim as he fought the controls, trying to remember everything he had been taught about auto-rotation. Luckily he'd already spotted his house and the field behind it below them when the engine crapped out.

Alice got his seat belt attached, forgetting the shoulder harness, scrambled into the right seat, and as she buckled herself in, began calling out their altitude so he would have that for a reference and could keep his full attention on flying the helicopter. *Her job as co-pilot wouldn't have a long tenure*, he thought. They were dropping like a rock and had about as much control as a brick with bumblebee wings.

When she called nine hundred feet as Cherub's nine, Mason yelled, "I should have practiced this more. We are going to come in hot. I've got too much airspeed."

"Aren't you a pilot?" Alice asked, panic creeping into her voice.

"No, but I did read a book on it once," Mason yelled.

He could feel her staring at him but was afraid to look.

When the aircraft approached a hundred feet, he pulled the nose up into a flare, using the last of the rotor's pent-up lift, and then they pitched forward, and he pancaked the aircraft into the ground in the field right behind the Admiral's house. *Perfect.* The tips of the rotors dipped from the sudden stop and hit the ground, chewing up small trees and brush like a weed eater gone mad. The chopper flipped over in a cloud of dust. *No gas, no fire.* He heard a shriek from the back just before his world went black.

Mason came to as he felt himself being pulled from the aircraft. Somehow, they had ended right side up. Alice and Mary Chen were pulling him away from the helicopter. Mary had a trickle of blood on her nose. Two other nurses were helping each other move away.

Alice stopped, made sure he was standing on his own, and grabbed him by both arms. "You were knocked out for about a minute." She held up three fingers. "How many fingers?"

"Blue eyes," he responded, looking at her steadily. "No. That's not right. Kind of a gray, with little green flecks."

He saw a slow flush begin in her cheeks. She dropped her left hand from his arm. The right hand, the one holding up three fingers, went to pinch her nose, and then she used both hands to rub her temples. She closed her eyes a moment.

"Jesus, you are brain dead already," Alice said.

Suddenly, Mason heard a loud, irritating noise.

"Law, why in the hell did you break that chopper?" Admiral Holloway yelled at him as he crossed the fence in his backyard and stomped into the field. "We could have used that egg beater."

Mason had to try a couple of times before he could find his voice again. There was a brass band playing inside his skull.

"Sorry, Admiral. Hell, I thought it was a pretty good landing, all things considered." He endured the Admiral's rolling eyes and unladylike snorts from the two nurses. "We walked away, didn't we?"

"It was a great landing," Alice said. "So great, we have a lot of brown to clean out of our shorts."

The Admiral looked at the nurse lying in a pool of blood in the back. "That one didn't make it," he said somberly.

Alice spoke up. "To be honest, the crash didn't kill her. We took incoming rounds from somewhere."

Mason interrupted the Admiral's response. "Folks, we better get the hell out of Dodge while we can."

"Why?" Alice asked. "Looks like we got away from the crowd. What's the hurry?"

Mason pointed back toward town. "That's the hurry." They could see smoke from several fires, and some were only a mile or so away. In the distance, as if to make the point, the sharp, staccato bark of gunfire came with the breeze.

The Admiral was undeterred. "I knew you were accident prone and will probably need a lot of care in the future, but kidnapping a bunch of nurses to bring along is kind of over the top, don't you think? Are you at least going to introduce me to the ladies?"

Mason stopped and shook his head—immediately regretting it. He had to wait a moment for the world to stop tilting. "You're a randy old goat, Admiral. This tall drink of water with the black hair is Mary Chen. The short one is Alice. She is the daughter of Major General Slade up at Fort Leonard Wood. That's what my visitor wanted this morning. To call in a favor. Requests from generals always roll downhill. I always seem to be the guy standing at the bottom wondering what in the hell hit him."

"Alice Slade," she said to the Admiral. She stood in front of Mason and held her hand out to the Admiral, all the while looking into Mason's eyes. "I was his co-pilot for about ninety seconds."

The Admiral said, "Did you help him land that thing?"

Mason broke into the conversation. "Actually, she did. I think she said 'Oh, shit' about fifty times on the way down. It saved me from having to do it, and that way, I could concentrate on my landing."

"Hey," she said. "You call that a landing? I've had a lot of good rides in helos. That was not one of them."

Looking at him critically, she gave him a little nudge, just enough to move him.

"You're dizzy, aren't you?"

Mason looked at her and said mildly. "A co-pilot could reach the rudder pedals."

Alice covered her mouth in mock surprise. "Oh? Short jokes? How original."

"Okay. Let's go, folks." Impatient but smiling, Mason was striding in a 'sort of' straight line toward the Admiral's house before he could be interrupted again. He was having enough problems with his brain without someone trying to help him talk.

TWELVE

WHEN THEY GOT to the Admiral's house, Mason stopped. "We need to get you girls dressed for the road. Those uniforms won't last long."

"Miss Chen is about my size," the Admiral said. "I'll see if I can find her some jeans and a shirt."

Mason looked at the Admiral. "I'll just bet you can. You're never too old, are you?"

"Okay," Mason continued. "Chen stays with the Admiral. Alice is with me." He looked around and saw the other two nurses huddled together and talking by the helicopter. "Let's move, folks."

As he walked toward his house, Alice said, "I don't think your clothes will fit me."

"My wife was about your size."

"You're married?"

They were crossing the back porch and entering the house when she said, "Wait a minute. Did you say...is my size, or was my size?"

THEY WALKED INTO THE BEDROOM, and Mason started rummaging through the closet. He pointed to a dresser. “Most of her clothes are still in there. Some are here in the closet.”

He pulled out a backpack and tossed it toward her. “Take what you need and fill it up.” Grabbing a bunch of clothes, he disappeared into the bathroom. When he came out, he was dressed in a dark-green polo shirt and cargo pants and a beat-up Cardinals ball cap. What he saw made him stop so fast he almost left skid marks on the floor.

“Uh…”

Alice was standing next to the bed in a lacy bra and barely there panties. Seemingly unconcerned about her near nudity, she stood holding the picture of Anne.

“Is this your wife?”

“Yes.” He couldn’t take his eyes off her. All of her. Five feet of ivory perfection. “Her name was Anne.” *Brilliant repartee.*

“Was,” she said. “Past tense. From the way you are looking at me, I am pretty sure she has been gone a while. Died? Ran away because she couldn’t stand your jokes? What?”

Mason raised his gaze from her breasts to Alice’s eyes. “She died. According to the Admiral, it was some kind of strange virus. Took about three days, start to finish.”

Looking at the picture, she said softly, “I’m sorry for your loss. There were actually several hundred that died from that virus. We never got a handle on it, or really knew what it was.” She looked up at him. “She was beautiful. Honest eyes. You weren’t here when it happened?”

“No, I was vacationing in the jungles of Guatemala,

courtesy of your father, the General. He greased some wheels, and I managed to get home, but it was too late."

She looked at the picture a moment more and then put the picture down on the end table. Face down. He wondered if that was significant.

"Maybe I should get dressed?"

He didn't pretend to look anywhere but her body. "Not on my account," he said. "I've seen some women, but...damn."

"Are you over her?" She was looking at him intently like she was trying to read him.

Mason met her gaze again and nodded. "She let me go the other night."

Alice seemed to ponder that a moment, watching him, and saw he was serious. "Good."

"So," he asked. "A beautiful woman like you must have someone?"

"Are you applying for the job?" she asked.

He felt the heat start on his neck. *What the hell?*

"You're blushing? I don't think I've ever seen a grown man do that."

"Just trying to make conversation with a naked woman. I'm kinda out of practice. Sorry."

"Well, you are doing remarkably well," she said. "As you can see, I'm not the least bit shy."

"So," Mason said. "The guy?"

"This is a weird conversation between two people who just met."

Mason grinned. "Things happen fast in a war zone. Besides, you started it by asking about my wife. And you are pretty close to being naked in my bedroom. So, the guy?"

"Oh, alright. The answer is yes and no. There is a guy

named Kirk that I'm friends with. We date once in a while. I've known him for years."

"With benefits?"

Alice laughed and then held her hand to her mouth. "What, you think I'm a thirty-something virgin?"

"So, this ugly gnome Kirk. Would I know him?"

"Look, my father kind of set us up the first time. He was an Army Ranger and still does consulting, which is why he is not around much."

"Tough guy?"

"He competes in the Iron Man contests. So, yes, he is. I watched him once. He's big, smooth, and fast."

She continued. "Is this important?"

"Yes," he replied. "It's called threat assessment. Besides, I don't do anything fast. I like to take my time. Like the song. Slow hands."

Mason was still looking into her eyes, trying desperately not to lower his gaze. "So, on again, off again? Just doesn't light your fire?"

"Yeah, maybe. More like I've just never been that serious about anyone." She shrugged and said, "The way things are, I'll probably never see him again. If he lives, well, I'm sure he'll survive this. But I doubt he'll miss me."

"Well, if he doesn't, he has to be three kinds of an idiot."

When she shrugged again, he finally lost the battle. *Damn.*

"What color are my eyes again?" she asked, smiling.

He couldn't tear his gaze from her. "Kind of wrinkled deep-brown, shaded with blush pink."

"I think you've been out in the boonies too long." She leaned over to pick up a blouse she'd placed on the bed.

He sighed as his gaze lingered on her. Her panties were just as transparent as the bra, and he could tell she really didn't like body hair much. He took a step toward her before he caught himself. Turning and escaping through the door, he growled over his shoulder, "Too damned long."

As he retreated to the garage to fill his pockets with supplies, he heard her laughing. It was a good sound. There was not enough laughter in the world right now. He thought Anne would approve.

WHILE THE WOMEN were still inside, the men stood looking at the Admiral's shiny red F-150 short bed nestled in the Admiral's garage, the bed filled with sleeping bags, backpacks, and enough gear to outfit a small troop of cub scouts. Behind the seat were an assortment of handguns, shotguns, and a couple of M-16 lookalikes. On closer inspection, they were not 'lookalikes' at all. *Where did he get those?*

"Did you forget anything, Admiral? Because I think we have a little bit of room right here in this corner." Mason pointed toward the back of the truck bed next to his one duffel bag. "We could probably get some mortar rounds in here, maybe a couple of rocket launchers. Say, do they still have that old cannon at the courthouse?"

"You're enlisted, aren't you?" The Admiral never paused in his organizing. "I will bet you scored high in wise-ass school. You have no respect for your superiors."

Mason ignored him. "Where did you get all that armament? You could start your own survivalist store."

"Gun auctions. The only place you could still buy a firearm without having it tracked."

They both paused, and they heard a deep, booming explosion coming from the city. The sound of heavy machine gun fire followed.

Mason said, "The last gun show I went to, every purchase was recorded, and the paperwork was horrendous."

"Not a gun show. It was an auction," the Admiral replied. "When the government passed laws prohibiting gun sales, the auctions started. Loophole, I guess. Some were actually done on the barter system. Plus, if there were any paper trails associated with the trade...well, they had a lot of spontaneous combustion, I'm told."

Mason said, "Well, that's one worry you won't have anymore."

The Admiral shook his head. "You are wrong about that. The government will have all the records. They will be finding the owners and collecting."

"What government?" Law asked.

With the tone of voice he would likely use with a small child, the Admiral said, "The one that comes after the present one, the one that wants to control us. That government."

"Still won't happen," Mason said.

The Admiral looked at him. "And why not?"

Mason was looking toward the columns of smoke in Springfield. "I don't think anyone will be home."

"So, which one of these rifles do you want?" the Admiral continued.

"None," Mason answered, finally coming out of his reverie and looking over the assortment.

"Why?" the Admiral asked incredulously. "I'm disappointed in you, Law. I thought you were some kind of a trained killer, secret operative kind of thing."

Mason replied, "None of the above. I'm just a guy that likes to stroll around the woods and find things. And to answer your other question, I don't think I'll need one of those, but I'm sure there will be plenty around if I do."

"Are you that good, or just stupid?"

Mason smiled at him. "I've never figured out the difference. Besides, we need to avoid fighting with anyone and stay clear of people. We are not invading; we're trying to get away."

"I hope you're right, but I doubt it. Let's hit the road, wise-ass."

As they stood there, Alice and Mary came out of the house. Alice had found Anne's hiking gear and was dressed in half-top boots, jeans, and a tee shirt, with a long-sleeved shirt tied around her waist. Mary was dressed in jeans and a pullover. It was obvious the Admiral was the larger of the two.

Alice came up to Mason and handed him an aspirin bottle. He said thanks and then popped the cap and chugged a few. He'd seen Mel Gibson do that in a movie. Or maybe Bruce Willis. Holding them in his mouth, with an expression like he'd just eaten something rotten, he looked around.

Rolling her eyes, Alice handed him a water bottle.

"Baby," she said.

MASON DROVE a few blocks to Highway 160, turned left, and headed northwest. Or, north...sort of. Seemed easy enough if you didn't clutter your mind with thinking about it. The sign said 160N, but they were definitely going west. He and the Admiral put Alice between them, because she was small, and had to pack Mary in the back with the gear. The other two nurses, against protests from everyone, had stayed behind to try and rejoin their families. The parting between the nurses were tearful, and Mason was sure they wouldn't be seen again. But, it was their choice. The last thing Mason told them was to use his house and anything in it. He didn't think they would be coming back.

"At least we'll avoid all the traffic jammed up in the city," Mason commented once they were on their way. "It looks like they are insisting everyone come into the town but are not letting anyone out. It makes no sense."

The Admiral rolled his eyes. "Remember what I said about control?"

As he drove, Mason rubbed his stomach and wondered how the superheroes dealt with heartburn when they chugged all those aspirin. There were a few vehicles on the road, but mostly people just walking, most walking toward the city, but a few of them headed away. The best speed their vehicle could make was about twenty miles per hour.

Alice dug around in her pockets and came up with a granola bar. She opened it, slid the wrapping paper down to one end, and handed it to him.

"Thanks," he said.

She mumbled something, but he didn't ask her what she said. He was pretty sure he heard the word idiot mixed in there, somewhere. *If this is the one Anne picked for me, it could be revenge, not reward.*

Mason thought it strange that people wanted to escape the city just knowing the folks out in the country had food, while the people out in the country were heading for the city in the hopes of finding food. It was lunacy.

Their route needed to pass through Willard, and then Ash Grove before getting close to Everton, where the Admiral's daughter lived, all told about twenty miles.

Worried about gas mileage, Mason asked, "How much gas did you put in this thing, Admiral? The gas gauge is showing pretty close to empty."

"All you had, about five gallons."

"All I had? So, that's why my truck ran out of gas before I got to the hospital," Mason said.

The Admiral continued like he hadn't heard anything. "That should be enough for a hundred miles, give or take." The Admiral watched people dodging away from their truck. "We'll make it if you don't get something squishy caught on the bumper."

Right on cue, Mason whipped the wheel left, then right to avoid an entire family walking on the road.

"Or hijacked," the Admiral continued.

"Jesus, Admiral. Are you choreographing this thing?" Mason caught movement in his peripheral vision just as he heard the shouted warning.

"Watch it!" the Admiral called as a man came from the side of the road and tried to jump on the hood. He could not hold on when Mason swerved, and then they watched him slip beneath the front of the truck. Two solid bumps from the driver-side wheels, and Mason knew there was no point in stopping.

"Jesus," the Admiral said, looking back through the window. "These people are crazy."

Mason glanced past Alice to the Admiral. "Not necessarily crazy. We just have what everyone needs. Gas and supplies."

ALICE OPENED the sliding glass window on the back of the cab. She reached through and held her hand on Mary's shoulder for a moment.

"Mary, are you okay?"

"Fine," Mary shouted. "If we'll keep from running over people. From where I am sitting, that was not pretty."

Alice patted her on the shoulder. "If I can get these two stand-up comedians up here to tell me where we are going, then we'll get things sorted out. Just hang in there. We've had worse rides."

"Don't I know it?" Mary replied. "I remember one earlier today."

"Speaking of which." Alice turned to Mason. "Where are we going, and what are we doing? Kind of in that order."

"Well," Mason replied. "Right now, we're heading toward Everton, where the Admiral's daughter seems to have a farm. We are going to warn her, or help her, or something. Not sure what. Then I'm taking you to Stockton Lake to your father's retreat. Or bunker. Supposedly, you will be safe there."

Mary had put her head through the opening so she could listen.

Mason continued. "What we are doing is trying to get some distance between us and Springfield, because that whole situation is going to get real ugly. You can take what we saw at the hospital and multiply that to every part, parcel, and neighborhood of the city.

"Just bear with us a while longer," Mason said. "When we get our feet on the ground, we will, as you said, get things sorted out. I know you don't know me, and I don't know you, but I will try and help. I knew your father well, and this is what he would want. When I get you to a reasonably safe place, I'll get out of your hair, and you'll be on your own."

"What if I don't want to be on my own?"

Mason glanced at her a few times, trying to gauge her seriousness. Then he smiled. "I guess we'll have to talk."

THE GROUP BECAME silent as Mason put miles behind them. Foot traffic was now nonexistent, and they gave any vehicles they met a wide berth. What worried Mason the most was, even though they were putting miles behind them, the road was curvy and they weren't all that far from the city. Thinking of walking distance, or running, it was not far at all.

They blew through Willard and came into Ash Grove, slowing down for a blinking light. At least, it used to blink. He didn't intend to stop, just didn't want to get t-boned by someone going the other way in the large intersection.

He noticed a small group of people in a convenience store parking lot. As they approached, Mason could see a couple of men struggling with a woman. Groceries were scattered on the pavement, and two little girls were frantically picking up the spilled articles, casting frightened glances at the struggle. One of the girls turned and seemed to be trying to help a man lying on the pavement.

As he watched, the other girl tried to help her mother and received a slap from one of the men for her trouble. *Damn it!* He might have passed on by, but not after the idiot struck the little girl. A quick scan revealed no one else there to help them.

Cursing himself for a fool, Mason wheeled to the right and skidded into the parking lot, leaping out of the truck. In his peripheral vision, he noted that Alice, little Alice in his mind, had bounced out of the truck almost as quickly as he had.

As he walked toward the pair of men, he yelled, "Knock it off, you two. Let her go." He was aware of Alice coming up behind him.

Both men struggling with the woman turned to look at him and just grinned. One of the men looked behind Mason and said, "Good, more women."

The first man to come toward him was heavy in an athlete gone-to-seed sort of way. He was wearing a fishing vest over a faded tee shirt and had a sidearm strapped to his leg in a holster that had probably looked great in the Bass Pro or Cabela's catalog. The man didn't reach for the Velcro wonder but instead decided to take Mason barehanded. Mason went in under the clumsy swing and buried his fist wrist deep into the man's gut, right under the sternum. It was a short and perfectly timed punch. The man's breath came out in a mewling squeak, along with every meal he had eaten in the last week, as he folded over to pray to the asphalt god, kneeling in his own vomit.

"Take his gun, Alice."

Alice replied, "I ain't getting close to that mess!"

But when he took a second to glance back, she already had her foot on the man's neck, pressing him face down on his last meal.

Having dispatched the Cabela's wonder, Mason faced the second man who was struggling with the woman. The assailant was so confident in his buddy's prowess he wasn't paying any attention. When he did see Mason coming up on him, he reached for a revolver that was jammed into the front of his pants and fumbled the fast draw. The draw had probably looked a lot better in front of his mirror at home. Maybe even awesome.

"Bad idea, sport," Mason said.

Pushing the woman away from the man, Mason stopped the draw with his hand while the revolver was still in the man's pants. He eared back the hammer and the struggling man froze instantly.

"Take your hand off this pistol, or you're going to lose your balls, then the ricochet will probably come up off the pavement and hit you in the ass," Mason said.

The man slowly released his grip and raised both hands to shoulder level.

Mason stepped back, bringing the pistol with him. "Now, pick up your friend and get out of here."

He watched as the would-be bad man helped the other to his feet, carefully stepping around Alice in the process, and then walk shakily toward a battered, rusty pickup parked close by.

"Thank you," Mason heard the woman say as he turned to find the woman and girls huddled together with Mary over the man struggling to get his wits about him.

When the man looked at Mason, he thought the guy looked like the famous football player who got his bell rung as was running up and down the sidelines yelling, "I'm Batman!"

The woman was still looking at him and silently mouthed the words, "thank you" again.

"Looks like he got pistol whipped," said Mary.

Now that Mason had time to look, he noticed the woman tending the man and kids was wholesome looking, with long dark-blonde hair done up in a ponytail, cornflower-blue eyes, and exuded a healthiness that said, without outside interference, she'd live to be a hundred. She was dressed in a print sundress of multi-colored flowers, while the girls were in shorts and tees and looked like small duplicates of their mother. She was trying to hold the girls to keep them from crying, and at the same time, trying to deal with the shock of what had just happened to her husband and family.

"Do you have someone to help you?" Mason asked while Mary and Alice began to pick up the spilled groceries. "If that is your husband, he is kind of out of it. Can you manage by yourself?"

It took the woman a couple of tries to find her voice again. Finally, she stammered, "I think so. We were about out of food, so we thought we would..."

After a slight hesitation, she continued. "I didn't think anyone would try to steal our food. I thought we'd be safe. My husband and I were headed toward Springfield and just stopped for food."

"I don't think they wanted your food," Alice replied.

"What do you mean? What else...?" Her voice faded as she started to realize what Alice meant.

"Look," Mason interrupted, thinking this woman had probably never had a bad thing happen to her in her life. "You have to take your family and get out of here."

When she nodded absently, he continued. "Look at me." When she finally made eye contact, he said "Don't go to Springfield. Everything is falling apart there. It is falling apart everywhere. Find someplace in the country, away from people, and try to stay out of sight. It is your best chance. Actually," he amended, shaking his head, "it's your only chance."

"But my husband is a doctor. He wants to help."

Alice said, "He'll have to help himself first."

Mason then tried to hand the woman the revolver he had taken off her assailant, but she refused to take it.

"I wouldn't know how to use that. I wouldn't want it around the girls."

Mason shrugged. "Your funeral."

When she just stood there, he tried one more time. "Lady, you have to go now. Don't even go home, wherever that is. Just get away from the city."

"But my husband..."

"Your husband is coming around, but you have to think of the children now."

That comment seemed to get through to her.

Pulling her two little girls close to her, she went toward one of the cars parked near them, casting frightened glances at him on the way.

When he got back into the truck cab, Mary wanted to sit up front.

"Sorry," Mason said. "It is crowded, and there is more room up here with the mini-nurse sitting up front."

"Stop it," Alice said, smiling.

"Anne never told me you had anger management problems," the Admiral commented dryly.

"They shouldn't have hit the kid," Mason replied to the Admiral.

Yelling through the back window, Mary said, "We could have taken them with us. A doctor would be useful."

"No," Mason said forcefully. Then a little sadness came into his voice. "No, we couldn't."

When no one replied, he said, "Look, we cannot pick up every person that needs help. We don't have supplies for that sort of thing. If we do start picking up people, then soon we will be leading our own starving horde around the countryside. There won't be enough food for us, let alone a large group."

Still, the disapproving silence. Then...from the Admiral. "Those little girls sure are cute. Did you notice how they tried so hard to not be afraid...?"

Well, hell.

Slamming on the brakes, he whipped into a U-turn and shot back toward the parking lot.

"Hey," Mary yelled from the back of the truck. "I'm not wearing a seat belt back here."

The woman and her children were still standing there, looking lost and confused.

Mason jumped out of the truck almost before it quit moving.

"Ma'am, if you want, you can follow us. The Admiral" —Mason looked over his shoulder at the grinning apparition in the passenger seat—"is taking us to a safe place not too far from here. Once we get there, you can decide what's best for you to do."

"I don't know..."

"Please," Mason said, looking at the children. "It's the smartest thing to do right now."

The woman looked at him for a moment. It looked like she was assessing him, not the situation. Finally, with a sharp nod of her head, she quickly herded her girls back into the car with her husband, and Mason led the two-vehicle parade west toward Everton.

They met a couple of vehicles heading toward Springfield, but otherwise the world looked peaceful, the way a beautiful spring day should. This was mostly brush and pasture country. Timely spring rains had the fescue growing belly high to the few cattle that were busy flicking flies and chewing their cud. It made him realize the seriousness of the hunger problem because he was sure the hills used to be dotted with them. The last few months had probably reduced the herds. He figured they would be non-existent in a week or two.

A few minutes later, the Admiral finally told him to slow down. "Turn right on the next road."

Looking at the narrow lane wedged between two fence posts and overgrown trees, Mason said, "That's not a road; it's a goat path. Look, Admiral," he continued. "I don't know what your daughter does out here, but if I hear one banjo playing, I'm outta here. That movie scarred me for life."

It wouldn't have been so bad if Alice had not started humming the theme song from the movie *Deliverance*.

THIRTEEN

MASON GUIDED the two-vehicle caravan down a tree-shrouded lane for about a mile. The lane was barely discernible, with twin ruts a tire width wide and the center covered in grass. The lane crossed rocky ground with no ditches on either side, just fence row and an almost complete canopy of leaves overhead. A creek meandered through the trees from the east, disappearing into the brush and trees to the west. Crossing a low water bridge with about six inches of water running over the top, they finally came out into a clearing.

A ranch style earth-home was nestled into a hill and surrounded by trees. The house was built into the side of a hill with only the front showing. From any other angle, it just looked like any other bump in the landscape. Out away from the home, and down a small incline sat a small barn, and what looked like a chicken house—judging by the amount of fowl running about. Farther down the slope, and in the only part that had full sun, were dozens of raised bed vegetable gardens.

When he stopped the truck, the Admiral bounced out

and walked toward the house. The woman following in the car got out with the two girls and her husband, who had apparently recovered slightly. She helped him over to the steps, and he sat down. Mason noticed Mary going over to talk to the doctor and then having the man chase her finger around with his eyes.

Universal to all children, the girls jumped out and started running around to get rid of pent-up energy—already deep into discovery mode.

A voice called from the garden area, and the Admiral reversed course and led them in that direction.

"Mason," he said. "This is my daughter, Angela Holloway."

A faded hippy walked from the garden. She looked to be in her early fifties. With her salt and pepper hair, thin flowered shift, and bare feet, she looked like she had just stepped from the pages of the *Mother Earth News*. When she took off her straw hat and bent over to use it to dust off the bottom of her dress, it was more than obvious she was braless. He thought it must be a clothing-optional farm because he didn't see any signs of tan lines. And there was enough time to notice. Unfortunately, and although she had a nice smile, her looks took after the Admiral. Someone trying to enlist you for a blind date with her would describe her as having a very nice personality.

"Hi," said Angela, holding out her hand.

"Well, what do you think?" the Admiral asked. "She's a beaut, ain't she?"

Before Mason had time to concoct a reply that wouldn't embarrass him, she said, "What brings you out here, Dad? Not that I don't want to see you, but you have never brought company before."

The Admiral immediately sobered. “The city lost power last night, and I'm betting it won't come back. Delivery trucks have stopped running, so food will be scarce. Things have taken a turn for the worse, Angela. It's 'bad scene' number one, two, and three on your list of the-end-of-the-world-as-we-know-it scenarios. We need to prepare.”

“Prepare for what?” she asked peevishly. “We've talked about this before. Our community is self-sufficient here. We have all we need.” Laughing, she continued, “Are we going to get that zombie horde the government warned about?”

“They actually warned about that?” Mason asked. “I guess it depends on your definition of zombie.”

The Admiral snorted. “Yeah, some low-level bureaucrat gave a press release about it last year. After that, I think he disappeared into a basement office in Adak, Alaska.”

Mason was just about to respond to that when he heard a vehicle coming down the goat path they called a road.

He turned to the Admiral. “Take the women and kids inside. Right now.”

Alice was suddenly at his side. “I can help.”

“No. I want you undercover. Now.”

“Yes, sir. I live to obey.”

Mason turned and watched her retreat to the house with everyone else. Then, perversely, she detoured to the pickup.

Starting to yell at her, he gave it up and turned his attention to the Humvee that pulled into the yard.

Two men piled out, along with an officer, while the driver stayed with the vehicle.

After consulting a printed paper with a picture on it, the lieutenant said, "You are Mason Law."

What the hell? Mason was startled, although he took pains not to show it. A stranger walking into a barnyard, out in the boonies, and calling Mason by name brought up so many questions he didn't know where to start. He didn't think he would like any of the answers.

"And you are?" Mason asked, stalling for time. All he had was the .45 tucked into his back waistband. He needed to get the soldiers close to him to have any kind of a chance.

"My name is Lieutenant Stark. Colonel Kessler, the post commander in Springfield sends his regards"—the lieutenant smiled at this and gave a mocking bow—"and needs to see you and Miss Slade back in Springfield. Specifically, Miss Slade. We will take her with us."

"Why?" Not that he cared. She was not going anywhere.

"Seems he wants her as a bargaining chip with her daddy the General. As a matter of fact, everyone here is directed to return to the city. And, since we are under Martial Law, you can consider that an order.

"You might be interested to know," Stark continued with a feral smile, "deserters from any military unit are to be shot on sight."

Mason considered that a moment, then ignored it. "How in the hell did you find us?"

"It was easy," Stark bragged, waving his hand in a deprecating gesture. "We were already at the hospital to pick up Miss Slade when the riot started, or whatever the hell that was. Then we followed her up to the medevac chopper but didn't have a chance to grab her. We had our own chopper in the sky above you. It has been tracking you since your takeoff from the hospital. Nice landing, by the way. It would have been nice if you had waited a few more minutes at your home. You could have saved us a long trip."

The lieutenant stepped close as he casually pulled his sidearm. "Now, about the woman."

The two soldiers flanking him had their M-16 carbines at port arms, and it didn't look like they were too sure about their mission. These were the older-style carbines with longer barrels. Law was pretty sure the soldier on his left would hit his barrel on his buddy if he tried to bring the weapon into play. They were just too close together. Law saw all this in a moment's glance before he turned his attention back to the lieutenant.

Lieutenant Stark chuckled and said softly, "They told me you were dangerous, Mr. Law. The Colonel warned me you were some kind of expert at surviving and to expect to lose a full squad of men if we tried to bring you in. Funny, you don't look dangerous to me. More like an old, used up—"

Mason's move was so casual the soldiers didn't suspect anything. The quickest move is directly toward your opponent, and his move was not even particularly fast. When the lieutenant had drawn his pistol, he didn't point it at anyone. Mason simply reached out, grabbed a handful of shirt, and pulled Stark toward him, twisting the gun away. He then pushed the startled lieutenant away from him.

"Drop your weapons, gentlemen," Mason quietly requested. He made sure the lieutenant was staring right down the barrel of his own pistol.

As Stark's eyes widened to impossible proportions, Mason thought he was going to cry.

"Do it," Lieutenant Stark instructed his men.

The two soldiers slowly lowered their weapons to the ground while Stark backed away with his hands at shoulder level.

A metallic coughing sound was heard, then the sound of a ricochet punching through the door of the Humvee, narrowly missing one of the standing soldiers. That sound was followed by the rattle of ejected brass hitting the truck cab. He glanced toward the Humvee and was surprised to see the driver hanging out the door, dead from a head wound. *Alice?* In the time spent talking with the lieutenant, she had found Mason's duffel bag with the M-4, assembled it complete with a sound suppressor, and taken out the driver. *Impressive.*

The three soldiers looked over at Alice like their chins were pulled by the same string. All they saw was both her eyes staring at them over the top of the M-4.

This was a new wrinkle. The beautiful girl he was getting all warm and fuzzy about had the coldest set of blue eyes he'd ever seen. Definitely not what he would want staring over gun sights at him.

"Mary," Mason shouted. "Would you come out here and be so kind as to relieve these men of weapons and ammo? Also, anything else you might think of as useful? And don't get between them and Alice."

Mary came out of the house and paused to look at Alice, shook her head and then commented, "Well, it didn't take you long to revert back to your old ways, did it, Alice?"

"Are you going to kill us now?" Stark asked, clearly nervous. "Please don't kill us."

Mason ignored Stark's question. After Mary finished, he herded them back toward their vehicle. "You boys can move along now. When you get back to base, give this Colonel Kessler a message for me."

Once he decided they wouldn't be killed, Lieutenant Stark's bravado returned, and he was nearly too mad to speak. He finally squeaked out, "What message?"

"Tell him to leave us alone. Tell him that a colonel can die as easily as a private. Is that clear?"

"You people killed a soldier in the United States Army, and now you are threatening the officer in charge of this region? I'll have you know, the United States Army..."

Mason calmly reached out and slapped him. Stark went to one knee from the force of the blow and then struggled to his feet with the help of one of his men.

"Are we clear?" Mason repeated coldly.

Lieutenant Stark stared at him a moment before replying, and Mason could see something wild in his eyes like there was an insanity just waiting to break out.

"Crystal," the lieutenant said.

AS THEY WATCHED the Humvee head back down the road, Alice came walking over carrying his M-4.

"Thanks," Mason said. "That was a good job of covering for me. Why didn't you just grab one of the rifles out of the cab?"

Alice gave him a look up and down, finally meeting his gaze. "I liked yours better."

"I don't like it that a soldier was killed," Mary interjected. "It's not right. This is getting way out of hand. You should not have done that, Alice. I thought you left that attitude in Afghanistan."

"Bite me, Chen. That guy wanted me, not you, so just drop it."

Mary started to open the argument with Alice, but Mason interrupted.

"I'm thinking some other things are at play here." He still could not rectify the notion that this colonel in Springfield would give a rat's ass about their whereabouts. He would have trouble enough just keeping the lid on the city.

"I wonder what he's doing that he thinks Slade will disapprove of."

Mary grudgingly commented, "Look, I am sorry to be so snappy, but I just don't see the need for this. Other than the hospital mob that got out of hand, no one has tried to harm us at all. There is just no need of this...this killing."

Mason said, "No one has tried to hurt us because we are out ahead of them. They will be coming."

"Well, I don't believe that. But, thanks for getting us out of that mess at the hospital."

Alice shifted the M-4 to her left hand. "Me, too."

"May I have my weapon back now?" Mason asked.

"No," Alice replied, drawing out the word and slinging the weapon around to her back with the muzzle pointed down. Out of sight, out of mind. She acted like he had asked for her favorite toy.

"I need this."

He realized that the weapon gave her comfort, like a favorite blanket as a child.

"Then you need to cinch up the sling a little more. The muzzle may drag the ground." He was smiling when he said it. After all, she was armed.

"Oh my, another short joke?" She batted her eyelids at him. "I mean, like, wow."

Alice stepped close to him. Something about her excited him. He didn't know if it was her perfume, the smell of gunpowder, or just the smell of...her.

He cleared his throat. "Well, I guess you ladies are welcome. I'm glad I could help." *Anne, you gotta help me here.* "And, thank you."

"For what?" Alice said.

"I won't have to kill myself now."

"Pardon?" They both spoke together.

Mason grinned. "Long story."

FOURTEEN

MASON HAD that quivery feeling that had never failed him before, that feeling that felt like spiders running up and down his neck and left him with a queasy feeling in his stomach. It was a simple message from deep inside. This feeling held true from desert to jungle. Get out, it said, and get out now.

He looked at Lieutenant Stark's sidearm, blew some dust off it, and checked the chamber. The toy soldier didn't even have one in the pipe. How could he not know that? Why would he attempt to take in Mason and everyone with, basically, an unloaded gun? Was Stark that inept?

Mason racked back the slide and then hit the release to slam home a round. Now, the gun was loaded. Since it was a .45, like his own, he thumbed the safety and stuck it in his belt.

Alice had come to stand next to him. "You know, with a pistol stuck in your belt behind your back and another one in the front, someone could hit you just right and you'd take off like a rocket?"

He grinned at her. He laughed at the joke but appreciated the hidden context. Hollywood notwithstanding, one gun stuck in your belt was bad enough, and two was asking for disaster. "You're right."

Tossing the pistol to Chen, he said, "Mary, take this and the rest of the weapons and start loading the truck. We need to bug out of here pretty damned quick."

When she left, Alice looked up at him. "What's the matter?"

Mason was staring at the tree line a couple of hundred yards away. "I don't know. Something."

"My spotter would get that way when the bad guys were trying to flank us," Alice said.

"Sniper?" he asked.

"Sort of. More like an ambush buster. We just shadowed the squad and gave them support if they needed it."

"Let's take a walk around. I don't suppose you will give me the M-4?"

Alice looked at him like he had two heads. "Uh…no?"

"What if I can find you something with a longer barrel? Like a 30.06 deer rifle and scope?"

"Nah. If the bad guys are that far away, we can just disappear. Besides, this ain't the desert. Too many friggin' trees."

Mason chuckled. "I like the way you think, Alice."

THEY WALKED the perimeter of the cleared-off area, past all the raised garden beds and outbuildings. There were a couple of milk cows grazing peacefully in long grass. For a split second, Mason thought someone was trying to sneak up on them through that grass, but then saw several miniature black and white goats jumping around and doing whatever goats do. He didn't see anything strange, other than a huge red rooster trying to herd two hens together so he could jump on their backs. It looked like job security, because from the way the hens were acting, that rooster was in for a long day.

"There is a lesson in that," Alice said, pointing at them with a snicker. "One at a time."

"If they would cooperate, it would work." Mason smiled as his gaze swept the area.

"Yeah, but that is the point, is it not? We never cooperate." Her eyes were as busy as his, scanning the tree line.

"We still talking chickens, Alice?"

"Nope," she said in a matter-of-fact tone. "Not unless you are denser than I think you are. I'm a direct kind of woman. I like you and don't ask me why. If my father trusts you, that is good enough for me. So, if you're interested, I am available. Simple as that."

"Hey. We just met today. You don't even know me. And, besides," he said chidingly, "you already have a guy."

"Had a guy, Mason. Had." She thought for a moment. "It is a well-established fact that in times of extreme trouble, like war, or whatever we wind up calling this, decisions of the heart are made very quickly. You're right; I don't know much about you. But I know enough. I know what is coming, Mason, and it is not going to be pretty. I have already made the decision that it will take most people days or weeks to come to. Unfortunately, a lot will die while they are trying to figure out what to do."

She continued. "Mary is like that. She is an idealist. For a while, anyway, it is everyone for themselves, and the devil takes the hindmost. If there is martial law, and the local military units are trying to herd everyone into the city, there just can't be a good reason for that. So, while we are dodging and weaving, trying to stay alive, you're going to need a woman, sooner or later, and she needs to be someone you don't have to worry about protecting all the time. I'm just putting my bid in to be your partner."

"What about your boyfriend?"

"He is not here, Mason. And, like you said, no fire. It was just a lukewarm relationship."

Mason smiled. "Do I get dinner first? Chocolates? Flowers?"

She grinned at him. "When there is time..."

"And if I am not interested?"

Alice put her hand on his arm. "One of the things I already like about you is that you are a terrible liar. You could have lied to me about my father's chances of survival. You didn't. You couldn't. That shows character. You could have jumped me in your bedroom. Lord knows I tempted you well enough. You didn't. That shows character. So, I already know you're interested."

She continued with a laugh, "Hell, Mason. A woman can tell. I look in your eyes and all I see is me in a tent, out in the middle of the woods somewhere, with six kids running around."

"Only six? Did I take time off for something?"

Alice's rejoinder was cut short by the sound of gunfire. They could hear the impact of heavy slugs into the fiberglass of the pickup and old car, followed by a strangled scream—cut off by another burst of gunfire.

As Mason and Alice rounded a small barn, they could

see a body down next to the pickup and smoke dissipating from the tree line opposite.

"Cover!" Mason shouted as he broke left toward the trees. He could hear Alice hosing down the tree line, expending a full thirty-round clip in three-round bursts. The firing stopped just as he hit the trees and he never stopped. Anger was driving him as he weaved his way through the brush and trees.

Bursting into a small clearing, he saw two men in camo crouching down behind an old fallen tree trunk. Both were pointing assault rifles toward the house. They whirled in surprise as he came into the clearing.

Even as he recognized the men as the soldiers that accompanied Lieutenant Stark, he shot one just above the V-neck of his jacket, notching his throat and blowing out his spine. The other tried to bring his gun around, but Mason was on him too quickly. He swept the barrel of the man's rifle away with his left hand and hit the man between the eyes with the butt of his .45. The man went down hard, clutching his bleeding forehead.

"Why are you shooting at us?" Mason asked in a voice calmer than he felt.

The man coughed a couple of times. "Stark told us to keep you pinned down until he could get back with reinforcements."

"Bullshit! If that were the case, you would have fired some warning shots at the house. What are you doing?"

The man didn't answer, and Mason kicked him in the ribs. Hard.

"Okay. Okay," the man gasped. "We thought if we wounded someone, we could pick off more of you when you came out to help. As long as it wasn't the Slade woman, we were free to do what we wanted."

Mason just stood there, shaking his head. "I warned you."

The soldier started scooting backward in the leaves and dirt, holding his hand out and pleading, "Don't. Don't."

Mason heard footfalls behind him, and recognizing the pattern, asked, "Who was hit?"

Alice walked right by him and caressed the trigger of the reloaded M-4, stitching the soldier from his crotch to his head. She turned away from the twitching body and put her head against Mason's chest. He felt her shiver and looked down to see tears running down her cheeks.

"Two people already in one day. I thought I was through with this shit," she said.

"I thought you snipers were tough," he said softly.

"I never said I was a good one." Stepping away from him, she straightened and then sighed. "That Mrs. Pennington is dead. She and her two kids were outside. The kids made it into the house. I guess they were bringing in supplies."

Shaking his head, Mason said, "I guess she was just snake bit. Bad luck. But if we hadn't brought them with us, she might have lived."

"Or, maybe not," Alice said quietly.

"Yeah, maybe not." They stood silent for a moment. Even standing in the middle of death, he noticed that Alice seemed to fit against him really well. Too well. He gently pushed her away.

"Wait a minute," he said. "Bringing in supplies? Not bringing them out? Dammit!"

Mason and Alice collected the mens' weapons and ammunition, then left the bodies where they lay. The man he had shot in the throat was small, so Mason stripped off his vest and handed it to Alice.

"Think this will fit you? There is not much blood on it."

Alice took it with two fingers and looked at it distastefully. "It will be a little loose, but okay." She searched all the pockets, finding everything from extra ammunition to granola bars.

"Wow," Alice said. "These guys were top of the line. I got a fire starter, water filter, tasteless survival food, and" —she held up two pistol ammunition clips—"nine mil ammo for a non-existent pistol." She looked disgusted as she finished searching all the pockets and put on the vest.

"Well, hell," she said.

"What's the matter?" Mason asked.

"No cigarettes."

"Good. Bad for your health."

Alice gave her patented un-ladylike snort. "Yeah, like I live in such a healthy environment."

He had to give her that one.

"Hey, Mason. Can you help me zip up the front of this?" Her attempt at looking coquettish was enough to elicit a smile from Mason.

Mason knew most people would think it odd that the two of them could trade quips while standing next to two dead bodies, with another just a few hundred feet away, but he knew the answer to that one. Either nurse or soldier, in Alice's case both, you do get used to it. No one likes death, or even seeing people injured, but when you see it enough, you can at least hide it away in one of the closets in your mind and slam the door. Besides that, your body is full of adrenaline, and your mind is just really, really glad that it is not you lying there.

Alice was speaking to him again. “Hello? Earth to Mason. Where did you go, buddy?”

He shook himself out of his reverie and said, “Let’s get back, Alice. We’re burning daylight.”

Mason loaded himself down with the extra weapons and gear while Alice kept guard with the M-4. He dumped the rifles into the back of the pickup and then turned to check on Mrs. Pennington.

Alice was already kneeling down, using her fingers to gently brush hair and dirt from sightless eyes, when Mason kneeled beside her. She looked at him with tears running down her cheeks. “I hate this. I really, really hate this. It’s not fair.”

“It never is, Alice,” he said softly. “This is why I want to get out of here. Dodge and weave.”

Rummaging around in the Admiral’s pickup, he had found a pistol to match the nine mil clips Alice had found. He pulled her to her feet. His left hand was in the vee-neck of the vest, his knuckles brushing against her breasts.

He seated the pistol into the holster that was part of the vest, and he said, “Look, keep it together. This is not over. Stay out here undercover and keep watch. I need you, Alice. Okay?”

“Yeah, Okay.” Then she said forcefully, “Okay. Alright? I got it.”

MASON LEFT ALICE OUTSIDE, behind the cover of the vehicles, to keep watch. He felt stupid and guilty that he had not left someone on watch in the first place and should have known that Stark wouldn't give up so easily.

When he saw all the supplies piled in the middle of the floor, he stopped. "What's going on?"

Mary and the Admiral both tried to talk at once. Mason silenced them by holding up his hand and then pointed to Admiral Holloway.

"Look, this is the perfect place to fort up and ride this thing out," Holloway said. "We decided it is better to stay here."

"We? Did that include Alice and me?"

Mary interjected, "You had already latched on to Alice and left."

Mason looked at her for a moment, mentally shaking his head. "And when shots were fired, instead of grabbing a weapon to help, you grabbed the good doctor?"

"His wife was already down, and we knew you were out there. Nevertheless, all of us left in here decided. I already knew what you would say. You just want to cut and run, and kill anyone that gets in our way. Besides, Alice will go along with whatever I say." Mary had gone back to consoling Dr. Pennington, who was huddled with his two children. "We have food, water, and shelter. That is what we need to survive. And this place is defensible if need be."

"No, it is not. You just proved that with Mrs. Pennington," he said. "And we'll be sitting ducks when more troops get here."

Mary stood rigidly facing Mason. "More troops? You mean that was the Army out there? Did you kill them? Are you crazy? We should have gone with them like they wanted in the first place. Martial law just means they are in charge. We have to do what they say. It does not have to be bad. You have no right to fire on our armed forces."

"Look," Mason said. "Your precious army just murdered his wife and tried to kill her children for no other reason than to try and draw you outside so they could kill you. When they start shooting unarmed civilians, then we have every right to defend ourselves. We still have a constitution and that is a very big part of it. They forfeited any rights to authority they might have had by that act."

The Admiral spoke up again. "Mason, I'm sorry, but it has to be this way. I am too old to run. You know that. And my daughter refuses to leave. This is her home. Besides, our vehicles are shot to rag dolls and probably wouldn't last a mile. I know you think this is a wrong move, but you are outvoted, son."

Mason looked at all of them. He saw determination in their faces.

"If we run, we can try and avoid a confrontation. You say you don't want any more killing, but by staying here, you are forcing that to happen. Actually, you are guaranteeing it will happen."

"When people come," he continued, "and they will come, are you prepared to kill them? Men, women, and children?"

Mary said, "We all believe they will pass on by...that's if anyone comes at all. I don't think they will. If they do come, we will tell them there is nothing for them here. We sit tight."

"Look, folks. We should leave and avoid confrontation. It is a good bet that a lot of people are going to die, but it does not have to be by our hand," Mason said. "We don't have enough bullets for the number of people that will be coming."

"You're crazy. My job"—Mary nodded toward the doctor—"and his job is to help people. Not to kill everyone we meet just so we can feel safe."

"But, by staying here," he argued, "you are ensuring just that."

"I don't believe that."

As he was about to turn, Mary said, "Wait a minute. We need to collect the body and bury her."

He turned to look at her, then at Dr. Pennington. Sighed. "No."

"What?" they both said.

"Look at it this way. Anyone coming up on this place will possibly find the bodies of the soldiers but will surely see her body out front. It may help them to believe that there was a fight here and that we've cleared out. After all, any civilized person would take care of their loved ones. That is...if they were still here."

"But..." Mary tried again.

"I'm sorry," Mason said. "It's a long shot, but she is doing us more good right where she is. If we last out the night, we'll take care of her. Besides, that is just her shell out there. Dr. Pennington, you should know that. Whoever she was is gone, and you want to remember her as she was, not the way she looks now. Keep her alive in your memory. I really am sorry."

Mason walked out onto the porch. He could see smoke rising over the trees, maybe a mile or two away. Looking around, he saw several columns of smoke in the distance, all located between them and Springfield. *Well, hell.*

"So," Alice said. "I see you just met steamroller Chen."

"Yeah."

"She always gets her way, but she is not always right. Just so you know, if you decide to leave, I'll go with you."

"Why?" Mason asked. "Alice, like I said before, you don't know me."

"Just call it a snap decision," Alice said. "So, we going or staying?"

Mason shook his head. "I'll stay for now."

"I figured. See? I know you better than you think."

Mason stood next to her, looking out into the trees. "Not to change the subject, but do you remember why those brave souls stayed and died at the Alamo?"

"Um, they were surrounded by the Mexican army?"

"Not at first. They could have left. No, they were fighting a rear-guard action, buying time for the Texans to raise an army. Their actions helped save Texas as a republic."

"And your point, Mr. Trivia?"

"I'm just wondering why we want to make a last stand here. What will our dying achieve?"

Alice said, "There is no back door to this place, is there? I haven't been inside, but these earth homes usually have only one way in and out."

"I'm just speculating anyway," Mason said. "I don't think anyone in there would split during a firefight and leave us holding the bag."

"Well," she said. "I doubt the Admiral will run, and Chen was Army, regardless of her ideology. I just can't see it."

Alice paused a moment. "I heard what you said in

there. Are you really going to leave Mrs. Pennington out there?"

Mason shook his head. "Nah. I just said that to pull their chain. I was losing badly in there. About dark," Mason continued. "We'll bury the dead. The Admiral can officiate. I'll dig and stand guard."

"When do you think we'll start getting people?"

He thought for a moment. "I can't see it before late tonight or early morning. Maybe not until tomorrow. There are fires all around us, probably from farmhouses."

"How do you think it will go?" she asked.

"We'll get the forerunners first, people with gas and vehicles. They'll be scattered and if they happen to stumble onto us, might listen to reason and leave."

"And, after them? What happens then?"

"The main crush of people will come. They are the ones who can't take care of themselves and will be desperate. They will come slower—men, women and kids, carrying bundles and packs. They will be hungry and scared."

"What happens when they get here?"

"We will have to fight."

"But why? They're just people."

"Alice, those people will be starving. Their children starving. They don't even know how to catch and clean a rabbit, much less deer or cattle. Their only option is to take what other people have. Don't expect a reasonable conversation with these people. It is an us or them scenario."

"What if we just give up and let them have what we have?"

"They will kill us."

Alice glared at him. "I'd kind of like to prevent that."

"Then we have to kill enough of them that they give up and pass us by."

"Is that possible?" Alice asked.

"I don't think so. That is why I want to leave. Think about it. Women and kids. Most unarmed, but coming like army ants. There will be men in charge who will think nothing of putting them out front, knowing we won't shoot them. Then, when they get close enough, they will rush us. When that happens, it will be fight or run, and they will be standing in our escape route."

"Well, hell," Alice said.

"Amen."

"I could really use a cigarette."

FIFTEEN

COLONEL KESSLER SAT at his desk going over his latest reports. His attempt at bringing everyone into the city was failing. He didn't have enough troops to seal the town off, and he was losing people in droves, including his own soldiers. Word had come that all the streets were jammed with people and the death toll was mounting. With a sudden jolt of prescience, he understood what must have happened to Major General Slade in Fort Leonard Wood.

He jumped up from his chair when the door to his office burst open. A young corporal in full battle gear literally skidded into the room.

"Colonel!" he shouted. "There are people all around the compound, and they're breaking down the fences. What should we do?"

Before the Colonel could speak, he heard automatic weapons open up outside. The deep-throated rumble of a .50 cal machine gun started and then abruptly shut off.

"I called for a chopper half hour ago," said Colonel Kessler. "Where is it?"

"There won't be a chopper, sir."

"What?"

"No fuel, sir."

Colonel Kessler turned pale as he sat back down at his desk and pulled his sidearm. Outside, it sounded like the entire compound was being dismantled piece by piece. The Corporal rushed out the door, firing as he went. Seconds later, his screams were lost in the pounding of feet as people streamed into the building. Once again, his door was slammed open as a crowd pushed into his office.

He stuck the barrel of his pistol into his mouth and pulled the trigger.

MASON RETURNED to the porch and asked Alice, "Please stay here and keep watch. I may be coming back with my tail on fire."

"Let me come with you," Alice said.

He looked at her sharply, knowing what she was thinking. "Look, I will not cut and run. My job, as I see it, is to keep you safe. I will be back. I just need to move Mrs. Pennington's body and scout around a bit. I can do that better alone."

"Chen can shoot. Let her watch, or the Admiral."

"No." When he realized he spoke more forcefully than he intended, he said, "Alice, I need someone here who WILL shoot, not who CAN shoot. I can't depend on them to not leave my ass hanging out there. Just hold tight and I'll see you later. Please."

THE FIRST SHED he came to had a sturdy wheelbarrow and a sharp spade. Mason took them back and loaded Mrs. Pennington's body on the wheelbarrow. He took her to the edge of the woods, found a natural, shallow depression, and started digging. As soon as he had a hole big enough, he gently laid the body inside. He sank the spade into the pile of soft earth. When he got back to the cabin, he stuck his head in the door.

"Admiral, I have the body laid out at the edge of the woods. Why don't you all say a few words over her? Do it quickly, and then get back under cover."

"But, I thought..." Chen started to say.

Mason just looked at her and went back out the door. "Alice, make sure they are armed when they go out and stay here for cover fire in case it is needed. I'll be out and about."

"Fine," she said grumpily, not looking at him.

He walked up to her until they were nearly touching. Reaching down, he raised her chin with his fingers. With a smile, he said, "Stop it."

She smiled back at him. "Go to hell."

MASON ENTERED THE WOODS QUIETLY. He knew the biggest danger right now came from the road and the lane going to the house. Picking a spot a few hundred feet out where he could watch the lane, he sat on a stump and listened. He could hear an occasional vehicle pass on the road. A couple of them seemed to be going west at a high rate of speed. The next one he heard was slower. He figured that one to be military and hoped they would miss the entrance to the goat path.

The wind was in the east, and before he had left the clearing, he'd noticed clouds filling in from the west. They would probably get a thunderboomer tonight with lots of spring rain. He briefly thought about the low-water bridge and the amount of water going over it. There probably was not enough runoff to bother it, but he'd better ask the Admiral's daughter, Angela.

Sitting in the relative quiet of the woods, he reflected on their situation.

Lieutenant Stark knew of their location, and that was not a good thing. The bodies of his two men that had been left to watch them were lying out in the brush, and Lieutenant Stark had promised to get back. In his mind's eye, he thought of the deteriorating conditions in the city, he thought it unlikely that the intrepid lieutenant would be back. With his attitude, the man was more likely to be stretched across the hood of some hunter's vehicle, like a trophy in deer season.

From his vantage point, he could see the front veranda of the earth home. Perfect for survival and self-sufficiency, it was useless as a defensible position. There was only one way in, or out. Once that was blocked, they were dead meat.

Like he'd told Alice, their first danger would come from those running in front of the mass of people. They would be armed and not above a firefight if you had something they wanted. But, with a show of force, he reckoned that danger would move away.

The second danger was the people fleeing the city, looking for anything they could eat or drink. As with any group of people, there would be a few strong-willed individuals who would try and control them—and would be successful to a certain extent. At least, until the ones in charge didn't produce food and water. There were a lot of homes and small farms in the country and those would be systematically stripped of essentials. It was just a matter of time until their little hole-in-the-wall hideout was found.

He looked at the area, trying to envision ways to defend it. Never a soldier, at least in the traditional sense, he could still think ahead and plan a few surprises.

As he watched the little prayer meeting break up, he stood and followed them into the lot.

"Admiral, we need to move some things."

The Admiral had seemingly aged in just a couple of days, and Mason felt his heart go out to the man. Admiral Holloway was a proud man, yet he was a man who could already see his future. Too old to run, too weak for a prolonged fight, he must still press onward. If Mason was any judge, the Admiral wouldn't sell his life cheaply.

Mason indicated the ground in front of the wide veranda of the house. "We need to get all the vehicles parked about a hundred feet from the porch, bumper to bumper if we can. That will give us some cover and keep a mob of people from rushing right up to the porch."

"Won't that give them cover for firing into the house?" Holloway asked.

"Yes, but we'll have to take that chance. Besides, the walls of this house will stop most bullets, but the vehicles won't stop a pellet gun. We need that buffer against a mass of people rushing the house."

"Can I ask a question that I really don't want an answer to?" Alice asked.

Mason looked at her, already dreading the obvious question. "Sure."

Alice swallowed a couple of times before she could

speak. "What happens when they start piling over the cars and trucks?"

"Then we start stacking bodies."

"Oh, shit."

He knew what she was thinking. "Alice, I'm hoping the women and kids will stop at the first defense. At that point, anyone rushing the house should be armed men and they will have made their choice. Okay?"

Alice turned sharply and followed Mary Chen into the house. Mason hoped she could persuade them to leave. The Admiral and his daughter Angela began moving what vehicles they had toward the front. When they finished, they went inside. From his vantage point, Mason could hear them arguing and yelling at each other.

He stepped into the house. "Stop it. This gets us nowhere. Admiral, I want you to divide up all the weapons and ammo between the windows. Everything needs to be loaded and ready to go, including magazines. There might not be a chance to re-load."

"Dr. Pennington, you need to place a table in one of the back rooms to use as an infirmary. If one of us is wounded, you need to get us back into action quickly, so prepare for that."

"Alice and Angela, I need you to fix a go-bag for each of us in case we need to cut and run in a hurry. Make it mostly food. I think there is enough in the Admiral's miniature cub scout camp to make that happen."

"What about me?" Chen asked.

"You?" Mason said. "You can drop to your knees and pray your stubbornness hasn't got us killed."

SIXTEEN

MASON SAT on the porch going over his weapons, while keeping an eye on the clearing. Everything was downslope from the house, so even with the vehicles making a barricade in front of the house, he could still see over them. The defender's small tactical advantage was that they held high ground. Emphasis on small. It wouldn't be enough.

A few minutes before, he had found a surprise inside. Angela had handed him a shotgun.

"Dad gave me this a long time ago. I never liked it. It kicks like a mule and bruises my arms."

The shotgun was a Remington with a modified stock and pistol grip. The barrel had been threaded and adapted with a Gator, an improved design of the duckbill, used in the trenches during World War One and the jungles of Vietnam. This deadly device spread the buckshot sideways and at close quarters was devastating. She handed him a box of twelve-gauge double O buckshot.

He guessed Angela wasn't the peacenik he thought.

As he sat, he heard someone come up behind him, and a hand on his shoulder. Alice.

"Mason, can you get out of here? By yourself, I mean."

He thought for a minute. "Maybe. Probably." Then he turned and looked at her. "Why?"

"There is no need for you to stay. You've done your duty. My father wouldn't expect you to carry this any further. Look, Chen is a friend, and I don't want to leave her. She's stubborn, opinionated, and can be a bitch at times...but still a friend. You don't owe me anything. Maybe we'll be okay if we just give up and join the crowd."

"Wrong," Mason said sharply. "I made a promise to get you to a safe area, and I will do that or die trying. And, for your information, your father, the General, wouldn't expect me to quit because the going is difficult. Actually, quite the opposite. I also have selfish reasons for this. While I'm getting you safe, I am getting me safe. Besides, it is more than that now and I think you know it. It has only been a day, but you have to admit it has been one of the longest days on record. Seems more like a week. Anyway, I think something has clicked between us. Maybe you won't agree, but that's the way I see it."

He continued. "What happened to what you said earlier? You know, the 'I'm going with you' speech?"

"I'm sorry. I'm just confused. It happens."

"Look, you won't leave Chen, and I don't want to leave the Admiral. Plus, I absolutely will not leave here without you. We're stuck here. I'm sorry, but I don't see a happy ending to all this."

The grip on his shoulder tightened. "Maybe we

should get some alone time to work on a different happy ending?"

Mason looked up at her. "Nah," he said. "You'd just want a cigarette after, and I don't have any."

TROUBLE CAME CRASHING into the yard in the form of three pickups. It was almost dark when they heard them coming, and it was sooner than Mason had expected. The attack was swift and hard. It was obvious the newcomers had scouted them out previously, because they drove right up to the barricade so they could fire over it. There was no conversation. No warning. Men began to pile out of the trucks and one man fired through a truck window at the house.

Mason rose up behind a heavy table he'd overturned on the veranda and yelled, "You men just take it on down the road."

Instantly, the men on the ground rushed the porch. *Stupid.* Mason opened up with a shotgun, pumping three rounds into them. He could hear firing from the house behind him, and the attack broke off suddenly, leaving several men writhing in their death throes on the bloody ground. The drivers took their pickups, loaded with a few survivors, and went tearing back down the lane.

Alice came out on the porch, looking around. "That was just...nuts."

Mason walked out and checked the men on the ground. They were torn up pretty bad and dead as dead can be. Chen and the doctor came out, but Mason just shook his head at them, so they went back inside.

"No fire and no lights," Mason called after them.

He stood looking after the pickups as Alice came to stand by him.

"Dammit," he said.

"What?" she asked, looking around quickly for more attackers.

"Those vehicles had gas, Alice. I was hoping we would get them all so we could use their trucks. Now, if we have to move, it will be by ankle express."

There was enough light left that he could see tears streaking Alice's cheeks. He put his arm around her shoulders and asked, "Why the waterworks?"

"It's the body count, Mason. It's really going up. A week ago, things were so simple. Hell, two days ago, things were simple."

As he started to answer her, he saw her eyes widen.

There were a lot of things they could have done to avoid this, but now it was too late. A solid wall of people was coming toward them: some men were on four-wheelers, and a few pickups were loaded with people. Mason wondered where they got the gas. Despite the few vehicles in front, most were on foot. He could see a few men chasing cows and the little toy goats with knives. Other people were just aimlessly walking around. The sight of them chasing the chickens would have looked great on video. It was easy to tell the sheep from the wolves, and he could only think they had staged this before they came.

Women and children, and a few older men, were in the front ranks. From what he could see, these people were not used to being outside and roughing it. They were dirty, with torn clothing, and not carrying much of anything. A few had backpacks or carried a duffel bag.

Most of the armed men were behind and off to the

sides, and it looked to Mason like they were actually driving the people like cattle. He saw men going in and out of the barn and outbuildings, but they didn't spend a lot of time there. It was almost a repeat of the mob at the hospital, except there were not as many of them. But there was enough.

Mason pushed Alice back inside the house. "Keep that door open," he said. "Once I'm inside, slam it and lock it."

When the people had advanced a little closer, he expended a couple of rounds at their feet. One of the shots puff-balled in a cloud of dust, and he winced as the other hit a rock and ricocheted into the legs of a woman who went down with a keening cry. The slow, shuffling advance stopped for just a moment.

I have to try. "You folks move on. There is nothing for you here."

He heard shouting out in the near darkness, and the mass of people surged forward. He didn't have the heart to shoot into them, so he retreated into the house.

As expected, they piled up at the vehicles. A few started climbing over.

Mason was standing at a window, Alice at another, and the Admiral at a third. Chen, the doctor and his kids, and Angela were huddled at the back of the room. He looked at the other two defenders.

"Okay, this is it. Try to pick out men with guns and take them out. Without them pushing, the others may quit. If they break in, try and retreat to the back rooms. Maybe we can hold out."

The surge of people stopped.

"What the hell?" Mason said.

The defenders waited a few moments, then saw a few

campfires start to show up in the area outside. Since it was about dark, it looked like they were about to have a barbeque. He could see people moving around the fires, totally unconcerned that they were in firing range from the house.

"I guess they aren't too worried about us," Alice said. "Mason, do you want me to take out a few of the men?"

"No, let them be. If they want to wait until morning, that just gives us more time to figure something out."

"Yeah," Alice said, glancing back at the others. "It is not like we are going anywhere."

He had noticed the Admiral and his daughter huddled together carrying on an animated conversation. Abruptly, he grabbed her by the arm and pulled her over to Mason.

"Guess what?" the Admiral said. "Angela has now decided it may not be a good idea to stay and try and defend the old homestead."

Mason just glanced at them for a moment, then continued to look out the window.

"It is a little late for that," he said.

"Maybe not," Angela said. She went to the center of the room and moved a table off to one side. Once that was done, she rolled up the area rug and revealed a door in the floor with a recessed handle.

"Every castle has a bolt hole," she said as she pulled up on the door.

"All this time," Mason said furiously. "And all the people we just killed, there was a back door out of this place? We could have left? Son of a..."

"Mason!" Alice admonished him, her hand gripping his arm. "Cool it. Please."

"Look," Angela said angrily. "I don't like you much or

what you represent. And I really didn't believe you at first. Then we were caught up, and it was kind of too late. I'm sorry."

Mason took a breath. "Okay. What is down there?"

"This is just a root cellar where I keep canned goods and store vegetables and supplies. The back of the cellar opens up into a small limestone cave. After about fifty feet, the cave opens out to the other side of the hill. If you want, you should be able to get away."

He considered a moment. "Alright. We need to check it out to make sure someone hasn't already found the tunnel. Angela, you show the way. I'll follow, and Alice, you have my back."

"Admiral," he continued. "I need you to watch from the window and sing out if you see any movement toward us. The rest of you get packs together for each of us and be ready to move in a hurry. Get the kids fed and everyone needs to drink a lot of water, then put some bottles in each pack."

They went down a sturdy set of stairs into the cellar. It was not quite dark outside, so there was just enough light from above to show shelves on both sides filled with jars and boxes. There were bins with the remains of vegetables stored from last fall: onions, squash, and potatoes. A little farther in, they could see a colorful blanket hanging on the wall. When Angela moved the blanket, it revealed an opening into the rock wall, and the floor was smooth and dry.

"This cellar was actually part of the cave..."

Mason held a finger up to his lips and shook his head.

He pulled Angela back next to the stairway and made a sign for her to wait there. Alice came with him to the entrance of the cave, and he whispered gently into her ear, "I'm going to chance a light for a few feet, and then I'll go dark. Don't follow unless you hear something."

He had her head in his hand and felt her nod. Handing her the shotgun, he made sure his knife was secure at his waist, and then with his .45 in one hand and a penlight in the other, he advanced through the cave.

As he advanced into the cave, he kept looking for water or wet limestone that would make the floor slick, but the floor and rocks to the side were dry. The floor was reasonably flat and dust covered, and he didn't see any sign of tracks.

When he thought he had gone about fifty feet, he turned off the penlight and stood a moment letting his eyes adjust to the darkness. He had always been blessed with good night vision, so he didn't have to wait long. There was a slight breeze blowing against his face, and if he didn't look directly at it, he could see a lighter portion ahead of him, so he assumed that was the entrance to the cave.

With short steps and keeping one hand on the sidewalls for reference, he eased up to the entrance. As he stood quietly and listened, his worst fear came to him on the evening breeze. He could hear whispered conversation all around him. In the dark, he could not tell much, but from the rustling of leaves and lack of any stars showing, he assumed the area was heavily wooded.

He was surprised that there were no campfires on this side of the hill, but he could still hear people moving around and murmured conversation. He put the .45 behind his belt as he skirted the rock wall to his left that held the cave entrance. A shape detached from the darkness and moved toward him. Afraid of an outcry, he was instantly behind the person with his hand clamped over their mouth. His blade was stopped in midstroke when he heard a voice calling toward him.

"Mom? Mommy?" *More kids. Dammit.*

Mason whispered to the woman, "No noise." When he felt her nod in assent, he took his hand away from her mouth. The kids were starting to cry.

As soon as her mouth was clear, she said, "It's okay, babies. It's okay. Be quiet, like we talked about before. Be very quiet." Miraculously, the children went silent.

His arm was still around her shoulders. She immediately grabbed his hand and put it to her breast. "Please. I will do anything. Please don't hurt us."

"Look," he said, unsuccessfully trying to move his hand. "I'm not going to hurt you. But I do need your help. We are just trying to get away. Are you hungry?"

"God, yes," she replied. "We're starving. We're all women and kids on this side, hiding from the people around the campfires."

"Where are your men?"

"The men with guns took them. What there was of them, anyway. There weren't many with us. When the mobs started going door to door in the city, it was terrible. They were killing people everywhere. Husbands and kids were shot. If a woman was pretty enough, she got to live." The woman shuddered. "Live to be raped repeatedly. I'd rather die. Anyway, a lot of us left. Some of our men may still be in the city, or are looking for us. I hope so. But we could not wait; we just had to get out."

Deep in his mind, Mason knew she was telling the truth, that it was inevitable. But it shook him to hear it firsthand.

"Look," he said. "There is a cave entrance behind me. It leads to a storeroom beneath the house. Even if they burn the house, the food should be ok. Now, I'm going to be bringing some people through here. Once we are safely away, you can go in and get food. I would leave it there and use it sparingly. It should help a while."

"The people on the other side are savages," she said. "If they find out we have food, they will kill us."

"Then don't tell anyone until the other group is gone. Just remember we'll be coming through here, and we don't mean you any harm. Don't start yelling."

The woman still kept his hand on her breast, and he could tell she was crying. "Can I thank you?" She squeezed his hand. "This is all I have."

Law finally was able to pull his hand away. "Just take care of your kids. And…good luck."

As he moved back to the cave entrance, he thought of how she offered herself to him out of desperation, and he never knew what she looked like. There was just a quiet anguish in her voice. And determination. He hoped she would make it.

A WHISPERED voice interrupted his thoughts. "Mason? Where the hell are you?"

"Here," he replied. With his hands extended to find the entrance in the dark, he ran into the leading edges of Alice. *Nice.*

She settled in between his arms and said, "Well, it's about time."

"Where is your vest?" It was really obvious she was not wearing it.

"I left it in the cellar. It was starting to rub me raw in places."

"Okay, but we need to get the others. I think we can get away from here," he said.

"In a minute. Just hold me." After a few seconds, she said, "Who is out there? I thought I heard voices."

"A bunch of women and kids, I guess. I talked to one of them. They are trying to stay away from the main bunch out front. She said their men were either taken away, or never made it back to them. Look," he continued. "We need to get the others and start moving."

"Alright, Mason."

He could feel her moving up on tiptoes and figured a kiss was coming. As he bent down toward her, he heard two thumping sounds. Before he could react, the cave behind them exploded with a huge gush of air and flying debris.

Mason and Alice were propelled into the darkness and he wound up on his back with Alice on top of him. Stunned and trying to take a breath, he heard Alice saying, "Oh, god. Oh, god," before he registered the pain in his right shoulder. He tried to move and realized something was sticking into him. As he tried to move away from it, and the pain, Alice whimpered again and he realized whatever had pierced his shoulder had to have come through her.

Alice suddenly went limp on top of him.

Mason started to rise up and, with the sudden stab of pain, realized he had hit his head when they had landed. With the pain came dizziness and nausea, and he lay his head back down. He could feel wetness creeping into his shirt and knew Alice was bleeding. Trying one more time, he rose up again...and then his world went black.

SEVENTEEN

MASON WOKE IN INCREMENTS.

The first thing he was aware of was Alice's whispered voice. "Mason, wake up. I need you. Wake up."

His world came back then, with the realization that she was still pinned on top of him. He glanced right, then left, and saw they were buried in brush about twenty feet from the cave entrance. He gently raised himself up, holding her tight against him, and turned sideways to put her on her right side.

Alice's voice was tight with pain. "Shit, that hurts."

On his knees now, he carefully looked around for people. All he saw was a lot of brush and trees. No one in sight. Apparently the explosion had scared them away.

He turned his attention back to Alice. A long sliver of metal was impaled in her left shoulder and protruded a couple of inches out the front. When he touched it, she winced and looked up at him.

"How bad is it?" she asked.

"I won't lie to you. It depends on your definition of bad."

"Dammit, Mason," she hissed.

"Okay. You have a piece of metal sticking through you. It's about a half inch in diameter. The big end is on your backside, so I will have to pull it out, not push it through. It could have been worse. It does not look like there was a lot of bleeding, so it missed anything major."

"Bend down here."

He thought she wanted to say something, so he bent down. Her hand went immediately to the back of his head, and her fingers went exploring. The back of his head was sore but didn't hurt a lot. She pulled her fingers away, looked at them, and there was no blood.

"Hard head." She smiled at him. "Now set me up."

Once she was sitting up, she looked around. "Wow. Looks like the whole world blew up."

Mason grimaced as he looked at the cave entrance. "More like we were shot from a cannon."

"What about the others?"

He shook his head. "I don't know. I'll look when you're taken care of."

"What happened?"

"I'm pretty sure someone bombed the house. I don't know how, but I'm guessing the Admiral and the rest were arguing again and weren't watching the front. Someone probably tossed a couple of charges through the windows. I think the force of the explosion pretty well rules out grenades."

"Who would do that? Is the military still dogging us?"

"I don't see how or why. But it could be soldiers who took some explosives with them when they bugged out."

She flinched in pain again. "Mason, we need to get this piece of metal out of me."

"I know."

"I wish we had some knockout pills," she said. "I'm not going to like this. I am really, really not going to like this."

"I know."

He examined the front of the metal tube and saw that there were no jagged edges. He kneeled behind her. The back looked much the same. He was worried about the part in her that he could not see. If it was fat in the middle and had jagged edges, pulling it out could tear an artery that was not damaged. But the wound going in didn't look any bigger than the object, so he thought they could chance it. He put his left hand on her shoulder, then grasped the piece with his right and tugged gently. It seemed to move some, so hopefully it was not caught on anything.

"Okay, Alice. Here's the deal. This piece of metal is smooth on the front, and the same on the back. I can only assume it is smooth in the middle. So, I'm just going to pull it out."

She was breathing hard, just from the pain of the jostling and movement of the metal.

"Okay." She nodded, close to hyperventilating. "That sounds reasonable. Just let me know when you are going to pull it out so I can brace myself."

"Alright. Are you ready for this?" he asked gently.

"No." She clutched her knees. Taking a couple of deep breaths, she said, "Wait. Not yet. Let me get ready. Okay? We'll go on the count of three. Go ahead and count to..."

Mason pulled it out. The metal made a sucking sound, followed by a spurt of blood.

Alice fainted.

MASON COULD NOT WAIT ANY LONGER. The bleeding from Alice's shoulder had stopped almost immediately. Still, he tore his shirt and made cloth pads for the entry and exit wounds. He laid her down, making a pillow with the rest of his shirt, and covered her with brush so if anyone was looking, they might not see her. It would have to do.

Everyone was gone from this side of the hill, and he'd had the impression last night that there were several of them. With a feeling of dread in his stomach, he went to the entrance of the cave.

Mason could only imagine how it went when the explosion happened. The wooden floor would have been blown downward. The shock wave of the blast had then followed the path of the cave, taking debris and Angela with it. She had been standing at the bottom of the stairs, and he found what was left of her body about ten feet into the cave.

There had been a slight turn in the path, and almost everything had bottlenecked at that point. If not for that bend in the cave tunnel, he and Alice would have been killed. Finding her, he tried to push the thoughts of the rest of the people in the house into the back recesses of his mind.

He worked a few moments, clearing enough debris that he could see farther back with his penlight. There would have been another thirty feet of debris to clear, with no reward that he could see. He regretted for a moment all the lost food, but there was not much he could do about it.

The bad thing was the loss of their personal supplies and weapons. They were back to square one. No food, no water, no medicine. The only weapon they had was his .45.

Backing out of the cave, he checked on Alice to find her awake and looking around.

He kneeled beside her and asked, "Can you walk?"

"I can try," she said.

He reached down and lifted her to her feet, being careful with her shoulder. She hissed a little with the pain but seemed to be alright.

"The cave is a shambles," he said. "It looks like the whole floor of the house was blown down through the cellar and out the cave." He hesitated a moment. "I found Angela about ten feet in. That was as far as I could get."

Alice looked at him with tears in her eyes. "I expect they all are gone, don't you?"

"Probably. I don't know how anyone could have survived that. We'll have to go see."

"I don't guess you have seen my M-4 anywhere?" she asked, looking around her in the brush.

Mason still had his knife and .45 with four extra clips, but it would be nice to have the extra firepower. He spent a moment looking around. He couldn't find her M-4 anywhere.

"Even if we find it, it will probably be broken. They are built like crap, anyway. Where did you leave it?"

"I leaned against the entrance wall just before I called for you."

He just looked at her and shrugged. "We're lucky it isn't sticking out of your back. We need to go on a scavenger hunt and do it quickly."

The hill the house had been built into was not all that big. They made their way around the base of it, and entered into the barn lot, much as they had the day before, and saw nothing but carnage. The barn and outbuildings had been burned. There were slaughtered animals lying everywhere. Pieces of each carcass were missing, but to Mason's eye, there was a lot of meat wasted. The temperature was mild for a spring day, and it wasn't hot by any stretch of the imagination. Flies were already working on the meat. He thought about taking some of it but simply didn't know how long the meat would keep. Food poisoning was bad anytime, but without access to medicine or doctors...well, he did have a nurse, but it was still problematic.

The gardens had been stripped of anything edible. As they walked up the incline toward the house, past the burned-out vehicles that had been blown onto their sides from the blast, and saw there was nothing left. The house was nothing but a debris field. The earth that had covered the roof was collapsed and made an effective grave for those inside. If there was anything useful left in the home, they would never find it. They both paused for a moment, looking at the house, and he knew they were both thinking the same thing. There was no use looking, and not much of a way they could without days of digging. No one could have survived the blast.

Alice leaned against him, and he put his arm around her.

"Chen," she said softly. "The little girls."

"Yeah."

She was crying now. "I always wanted some little girls of my own, so did Chen."

"We'll get through this," he said, although he could not put much conviction in his voice.

"Promise?" she asked.

Mason sighed. All those people gone. His friend. Alice's friend. Thousands were dead, maybe more than that, and yet they mourned these few.

He shook her a little. "Let's go, Alice. We cannot stay here."

EIGHTEEN

BEFORE THEY STARTED OUT, they made one more sweep of the area, looking for anything useful and keeping an eye out for people. When they stopped to look at the bodies of the two soldiers, an incident that happened a lifetime ago, it seemed, they both looked at them in shock. The bodies had been horribly mutilated. They turned away in disgust.

"They were already dead, Mason. What in the hell is that all about?" Alice shuddered after she spoke, trying to get the picture of the grisly scene out of her mind. "It looked like part of their legs were missing."

"Alice, I don't even want to think about the answer to that one." He paused a moment. "I know the answer—I just don't want to think about it."

"Don't keep things from me, Mason. Tell me."

He shrugged. "A small group of people moving around can live off the land a bit. If you get a group of hundreds, maybe a thousand...what are they going to eat, Alice? It's not like they can send out for pizza."

She grasped his arm and turned him to her and

pleaded with him. "Don't let that happen to me, Mason. Promise me. Bury me deep."

"I am not planning on you or me having to worry about that." He tried to be reassuring.

"It can happen, whether we plan for it or not." Alice unbuttoned her blouse and pulled it to the side, revealing her bare shoulder. "Look at this wound, Mason. Is it red around the edges? Is it oozing anything? Crusted over? If this gets infected, there is no way to stop it. I'll die, and you know it."

Something had been trying to surface in Mason's mind. It finally came to him when he looked around and saw the raised gardens that Angela Holloway had so meticulously kept. *Idiot!*

He grabbed her hand, the one attached to the good shoulder, and pulled her with him.

"Do you know what mint looks like?" he asked while he walked around the beds.

"What?"

"You know. Mint. Herbs. The leaves that you put in the pot when you cook." Mason had already found Angela's bed of herbs. Actually, when he really started paying attention, most of the beds had some kind of herb growing over the sides.

"Look, Mason." She was trailing along behind him. "I do several things well. I do one thing really well. Cooking is not on the list."

Grabbing a handful of green leaves, he stuffed them in a pocket.

"Come on," he said. "We have to make tracks."

IT WAS midday when he found what he wanted. Following a ridge line of limestone that looked like it used to be a streambed, he found a spring that was surrounded by brush and cedar. The pool of water was only a couple of feet across and seeped back into the rocks. The pool was full of watercress, but looked crystal clear.

Mason decided to make camp, even though it was early in the day. Alice looked tired and they had a lot of work to do. As she sat on a rock to rest, he looked around and decided their luck was changing for the better. Back against the wall was a pile of trash. Someone had used this as a camp before. The lucky find was a tin can.

He went back to the pool and stood looking around. He gathered some dead leaves and small dry sticks and dug out a small depression in the dirt for them. Once that was ready, he stood up again.

"What are you doing, Mason?"

He glanced at her. "I'm trying to remember how to start a fire. I flunked that in Boy Scouts."

"Mason?"

"If I can find some dry wood, I think I can do it."

"Mason."

"It will take a while..."

"Mason!"

If a whisper could be a yell, she had just done it with a voice full of exasperation.

He looked at her, startled. "What?"

She reached into her pocket and pulled out a lighter. Holding it out to him, she said, "If you were a real Boy Scout, you'd find me a cigarette."

His comment of 'you are amazing' just granted him an eye roll as he started getting things together.

Alice scooted down to use the rock as a backrest and was instantly asleep.

It took an hour, but he was finally ready. Starting the fire with dry wood to cut down on smoke, he'd filled the can with water and set it down in the fire. The fire would sterilize the outside, and hopefully the boiling water would do a good job of cleaning the inside. Once this was done, he got fresh water and brought that to a boil. He hated to do it, but he sacrificed his one plastic water bottle to make a little dish with the butt end. He put boiling water in it, then crushed up the mint leaves. With the butt of his knife, he mashed the leaves and made a paste.

With boiling water at hand and the medicinal paste, he was ready. The last thing he did was put the point of the knife in the flames.

Turning to Alice, he shook her awake. "Come on, Alice. I need to take your blouse off."

She looked at him groggily. "Not now. I don't feel like it."

He filed away the fact that this woman didn't wake up in a good mood. "I need to clean your wound."

Once he had stripped her down to her bra, he saw the wide elastic strap was going to be in the way. He gently pulled it off her shoulder to hang on her arm. As he did, the cup fell away from her breast. He could not resist.

"Damn, Alice!"

She glanced down and then met his gaze. "I had a whole different scenario in mind to show you these."

"I'll take a rain check. Just hang in there, okay?"

Using the remnant of his shirt, he used the hot water to clean around the wound, both front and back. Poking around in the wound, he could not find any foreign matter. The tissue was pink, with just a little blood showing.

"Looking good, Alice. I don't see any sign of infection yet."

"No streaks going out from the wound? Not white around the edges?"

"Not that I can see. I guess we need to close up the wounds."

She bolted upright, wincing in pain. "Is that why you are sterilizing your knife point? You want to cauterize the wounds? This isn't the old west, Mason. This wound needs to heal from the inside out. It needs to drain, not be closed up. I'm the nurse, Mason. Not you."

"But..."

Alice moved her shoulders, causing her breasts to sway from side to side. The movement caused her to grimace in pain, but he got the message.

"If you ever want to see these again..."

"I got it," he said.

"Good," she said. "Because doing that really hurt. We have to work on another way for me to get your attention."

He went ahead and made wet compresses with the mint and applied them to both wounds. Pulling her bra back up, he placed the strap to hold the pads of cloth in place. After that was done, he helped her back into her blouse.

"You rest," he said. "I'm going to look around some."

She looked at him and said, "Mason? Thank you."

"Anytime."

"Mason?"

"Yeah?"

"Food."

"You're really high maintenance, you know that."

Sarcasm was lost. She was asleep.

HE STOOD LOOKING at her for a moment. Looking but not seeing. Lost in thought.

Not long ago, he had a wife and perhaps a chance of a future. A few days ago, he was going to end it all. He still thought there was an intervention on that one. *Thank you, God, or thank you, Anne, or just thank my lucky stars.* Yesterday, they had food, water, and weapons. They had shelter, although that was a mixed blessing. They had the feeling of control over their surroundings.

Today? He had a girl he was really starting to like, the clothes on their backs, meager weaponry, and no food. Today, they had a true survivalist's nightmare. A nightmare because no one really wants the bad things to happen. Of course, preppers and survivalists had been writing about the possibility for years on the internet and in books. SHTF (shit hits the fan), and TEOTWAWKI (the end of the world as we know it).

There was one slight advantage. He was back in his element, and it was time to start correcting some of the problems facing them.

He pulled his .45 and placed it next to the sleeping Alice, along with the extra clips and her lighter. If something happened and he didn't make it back to the camp... well, it would give her a better chance.

When they came up on the spring, he had noticed a slight trail going up between the rocks of the bluff. Whether a game trail, or something else, he didn't know. But trails generally lead somewhere.

Following the trail to the top of the bluff, he could see the land around them. Back the way they had come, he could see smoke from numerous fires burning. The larger ones he took to be the small outlying towns, like Ash Grove and Everton. The smaller fires he supposed were campfires. Looking forward to the north and west, he didn't see much at all, except to the west of their position. From the map, one of those items he used to have, he remembered seeing a town called Greenfield over there.

Walking another mile, he crossed a dirt road and saw a house nestled in the trees. He almost missed it. The house was small and nearly concealed by trees, just a one-story building that resembled hunting cabins he had seen in pictures. Watching the house, he saw no sign of people. As hidden as it was, it just might have been missed. Or it might be occupied and become a trap. He settled down to wait.

After an hour of watching, he decided to check it out. There were no vehicles to be seen and there were no outbuildings to hide them in. So, maybe the owners were gone. No smoke from the chimney, so no cooking. Maybe. There was only one way to find out.

He circled the cabin once, looking for dogs. He found one, but it was dead. It was chained to a tree and looked like it had starved. Something must have happened to the owners, because leaving the dog chained up to die was way out of character for most anyone. And the owners must have been gone long before things had fallen apart. The place looked well-kept so that pointed to responsible people. *Strange.*

He peeked into the windows and saw no movement. Finally, he tried the door. It was locked. He went around and tried the back door. Locked.

Entering the cabin would be noisy. It was time to get Alice and the gun.

It took him about an hour to retrace his steps to the camp. It was nearing mid-afternoon when he quietly came down the game trail and into the camp. He walked right into trouble.

Three men and a woman were in the clearing, all facing toward Alice. She was still sitting with her back against the rock, but had the .45 in a two-handed grip. One glance told him the safety was off. The pistol wavered a moment, then her hand steadied. From where he stood, Mason could tell she was flushed with fever.

Mason stood with his knife held on the inside of his arm, pointed upward toward his shoulder. When Alice glanced at him, they all whirled as one. While they were all armed, their weapons were not raised. Dressed in fatigues and black shirts, they looked well-armed and equipped.

"Alice," Mason said. "If they start something, shoot the woman. I will take care of the men."

The woman looked at him, startled. It was plain that she didn't like that.

One of the younger men responded, "You're not even armed. If we start something, you will regret it."

Mason had been slowly moving toward them, closing the distance. Every foot he could get closer gave him a better chance.

One of the men was older, with close-cropped gray hair and chiseled features. He was the only one who seemed to notice what Mason was doing and had quietly moved back for every step Mason had come forward.

"Look, why don't you folks move on," Mason said.

"We are no threat to you. I have a sick woman that I need to take care of."

When the young man started to answer, the older man interrupted. It was easy to tell who was in charge by the swiftness with which the younger man shut up. The woman was glancing over her shoulder at Alice, seeming to measure her chances.

"Let's just everyone cool down a minute," the older man said. "Charlie, don't you see how ready this man is? Don't you see how he's holding that K-Bar? That's not just a toad sticker, it is an honest-to-by-God marine fighting knife, and I'm guessing this man knows how to use it."

"Stop," Mason said at the first movement from the group that started to back away from Alice. He didn't want to lose the tactical advantage that Alice held.

"Alright, let's just stand down, people." The older man was trying to defuse the situation. He held his hands up, waist high. "Look, man. We need to back away, and we will, but you need to let us. I don't think either of us wants this to turn ugly. There is no need for us to kill each other."

Mason looked at them a moment, and then nodded his head, and the people moved back. All except Charlie.

"Tolliver, I ain't lettin' this go. It's easy for you. You already got a woman. I like the looks of this one, and I want her."'

Tolliver tried one more time. "Charlie..."

Charlie was staring at Mason, his eyes wide with adrenaline, pumping himself up and measuring his chances.

It happened quickly. A fight between two assailants

rarely lasts more than fifteen seconds. This one lasted half that. It just needed a catalyst.

The heavy .45 wavered in Alice's hand.

"Mason," she said. "Baby, I can't hold..."

Alice fainted, and the sound of the .45 hitting the soft dirt was loud enough to be heard. When Mason glanced toward her, Charlie launched himself at him. When Charlie got to Mason, he seemed to do a flip around Mason's arm, then hit the ground with a solid thump. He didn't move, and what little dust that was stirred by the action settled on his unblinking eyes. The red stain just under his sternum didn't spread much because Charlie's heart had stopped beating already.

Mason seemed to have hardly moved and stood facing the others, his knife held straight down in his hand and blood dripping from the point.

"I didn't want this," he said harshly.

"He was a damned fool," Tolliver shrugged and said. "I would have had to kill him myself, sooner or later."

"I need to take care of Alice," Mason said. "Now."

"That shoulder of hers is infected," the woman said. "I could see it. I can smell it, although the mint is a nice touch. She needs medicine."

"That's something I don't have," Mason said, edging toward Alice but still on guard.

The woman looked at Tolliver for permission. At a nod from him, she un-shouldered her pack and dug around in it, coming up with a baggie that held a hypodermic needle and clear liquid in a bottle. She un-packaged it and drew off some of the liquid from the bottle. Quickly and efficiently, she bared Alice's shoulder and gave her a shot in the arm. Then she handed the bag and its contents to Mason.

"Antibiotic," she said. "It's strong stuff, so just give her a couple of CCs every day. It should help. And clean that damn wound."

As they started to leave, Mason asked, "Why?"

Tolliver looked back at him. "We're not all savages. Besides, I didn't like Charlie sniffing around my woman. You saved me some trouble. I don't know your name," said Tolliver.

"Mason Law."

The man stared at him a long moment, then said, "I have friends in the military. I've heard the name." He walked over to the dead man and nudged him with his foot. "You poor damn fool."

"Where are you headed?" Mason asked.

"Anywhere," Tolliver said. "Nowhere. We left the Fort Leonard Wood area, just staying ahead of the mob. We bypassed Springfield and then ran out of gas." He paused for a moment. "The men and women there tried to defend the ordinance at the Fort. They stood their ground. I'll give them that." He shook his head. "They didn't have a chance."

"Did you hear anything about General Slade? Did anyone get away?"

"I don't know for sure, but I'm betting the General wouldn't have left, no more than his people would leave him. Why?"

Mason nodded toward Alice. "His daughter. You're military?"

"Nah. Just Preppers. Used to be, a long time ago."

Mason made a snap decision. "North of here is Stockton Lake. There are some places to hole up there. It could be a start."

Tolliver shrugged. "Maybe. Maybe not. Right now, we

gotta boogie. Look. There are people behind us. A lot of people. They are moving slow, but they're comin'. You best be moving, too." He looked at Alice, and Mason could see the doubt in the man's expression.

"We'll manage," Mason said.

"No doubt you will."

"One thing, Tolliver," Mason said. "A couple of days ago, we were holed up in a house when the first wave of people came. We were lucky to get out alive."

Tolliver nodded like he already knew the answer. "They just kept coming, didn't they? Not enough bullets to stop all of them?"

"No," Mason said. "Someone was controlling them and they stopped short. They fixed camp, built fires, and ate a good meal. Everything looked kind of peaceful. Later, they threw a couple of satchel charges through the windows. If Alice and I had not been in a cave under the house..."

"Jesus," the woman said.

Tolliver and Mason looked at each other, a mutual understanding shared.

"That's good to know. Real good," Tolliver said.

"That happened with the bunch that is ahead of you. If someone is controlling them, there may be flankers or scouts out. Be careful."

MASON STRODE FORWARD and retrieved the .45, then stood listening for a minute, alert to the idea they might come back. When that didn't happen, he turned to Alice, putting his hand to her forehead. She was burning up.

Turning to look at the man he had killed, he quickly went through his pockets, searching for anything useful. There was not much there, just the short-bladed fighting knife that he'd attacked with and some change in his pocket. Where he thought he'd spend that, Mason didn't know. No ammo, no firearm. He must have been a latecomer to Tolliver's group.

Mason sheathed his knife and checked the action of the pistol to make sure there was no dirt in the slide, and then put the .45 in his belt. Bending, he picked up Alice and struggled up the bluff with her over his shoulder. Although she could not weigh more than a hundred pounds, it was going to be a long two miles to the cabin. He prayed it would be unoccupied when he got there.

With the antibiotics, she had a good chance.

NINETEEN

AFTER SPENDING a few minutes observing the area, Mason carried Alice to the cabin and sat her down on the porch. Then he kicked in the door. It took him two tries because it was a solid wood door, and heavy. If it were barred from the inside, he wouldn't have been able to do it. The fact it was not barred told him the place was unoccupied. That, and the fact that no one had shot them on the way to the porch. After carrying Alice for a couple of miles, he was just too damned tired to care.

He had time for a cursory inspection of the house before he moved a heavy chest in front of the door. After laying Alice on a full-size couch, he found the bathroom medicine cabinet. He almost cried when he found several tubes of topical antibiotic. He went to the kitchen and found white tea towels, then returned to the bathroom. He took the lid off the toilet tank and was pleased to find it full of water. Going back to Alice, he cleaned the wounds the best he could.

By now, it was fully dark, and Mason could not see much inside the house. There was a comforter on the back of the couch, so he gathered Alice into his arms, wrapped them both up in the blanket, and fell into an exhausted sleep.

MASON AWOKE with a lurch the next morning just as the windows had started to show the light of sunrise. He heard the noise that woke him...a scratching noise on the front porch. He glanced at Alice and she was staring back at him. Gently, he extricated himself from her, picked up the .45 from the end table and softly walked to a window. He then turned back to Alice.

"Squirrel," he said.

"I could eat a squirrel," she said quietly. "Fur and all."

Mason chuckled. "It would make too much noise to shoot it, and I'm not fast enough to catch it." He looked at her more closely. "You are feeling better."

She sat up straight on the couch and then stretched. With a grimace, she grabbed her shoulder. "Well, I was feeling better." With a helping hand from Mason, she rose to her feet.

"So far, so good," she said. "I don't remember much from yesterday. I'm pretty sure Mr. Grabby Hands and his motley crew didn't kill us, and I don't feel used and abused, so what happened?"

"They weren't bad folks," he said. "Well, all except for the one who wanted to lay claim to your body. He didn't fare too well."

"Oh, Mason. Did you kill him?"

For some reason, he could not meet her eyes. "Had to," he said. "Like John Wayne said in a movie, 'Conversation kind of dried up.'"

Alice was looking at him, and he could see emotion flowing like a ticker tape across her eyes. Finally, she said, "This is going to sound weird. But I'm sorry you had to do that. I am also glad that you did. Does that sound stupid? I just don't want to think of the alternative."

"Not stupid or weird. Crazy, maybe. We've only known each other a short time, so I can't judge."

He was amazed that she was crying. "Long enough," she said.

"Actually, they gave you a gift." He reached into a pocket and handed her the package of antibiotic. "The lady with them said two CCs a day. She gave you a shot yesterday." Reaching out a hand, he said, "I can do that now if you want."

"No," she said. "I need to clean up."

"The bathroom is down the hall. I think there is enough water in the tank for one flush."

"Oh, goodie. What about you?"

"I'll find a spot outside. I need to look around anyway."

When Alice closed the door of the bathroom, he went outside and took a quick look around. It looked like a normal spring morning; dew on the grass, birds singing, and squirrels barking in the trees, a soft breeze wafting through the leaves. *Yeah, right.* Seeing no movement outside, he went back inside to do a little exploring. The kitchen was first, and he could not believe all the canned goods and dried food in the cupboards. Just on a whim, he tried the light switch and was startled when the lights came on. Like he was guilty of doing something wrong, he quickly switched them off. *Where did the power come from?*

The next shock came when he discovered they had

running water. It was a jaw-dropper when he ran the water a moment and found they had hot water.

He went and tapped on the bathroom door. "Alice?"

Her answer was melodious and drawn out. "Yes. I'm busy?"

"Try the hot water in the bathtub."

He heard water running, and after about a minute, a delighted shriek. "Boy, Mason. When you pick a hideout, you really go first class."

A few minutes later, he was passing by the door to the bathroom when he heard her call out.

He stopped and said, "Are you about through in there?"

"I need your help."

"Are you decent?" Great line, Mason. Like you care.

"Come on in," she said.

He opened the door and poked his head in. "Whoops!"

She was sitting in the tub with her arms crossed over her breasts. With an exasperated look at him, she said. "I need you to look at my back. It stings like hell."

He came over to the tub, and she leaned forward. Her back looked like a connect-the-dots puzzle without the lines drawn in. It was another price she had paid when she shielded him from the blast. He could see scores of little punctures, like splinters all over her back. Now it looked like they were becoming infected.

When he told her what he saw, she said, "Well, fix it. The water is getting cold."

Eliciting a startled glance from her, he reached in front of her and released the lever to start draining the tub, then turned on the hot water. The water ran a minute while he was rummaging around in the medicine cabinet for tweezers and alcohol. Finding those items, he turned just as he heard her say something.

"What?" he said.

"I asked how am I going to adjust the water?" Then she said, "Oh, the hell with it," and dropped her arms from her breasts and adjusted the hot water so she didn't get scalded.

He just stood there.

Finally… "It's rude to stare," she said.

"I can't help it. You're a beautiful woman, Alice."

"Yeah, well, how about taking care of this woman's wounds? You can stare later."

Snapping out of his daze, he sat on the edge of the tub and said, "Promise?"

IT TOOK close to an hour to remove all the splinters of wood and slivers of rock (he guessed). Mason had to keep going out and checking the windows. He didn't want any surprises. There was not much hot water left when they were done.

"Okay," Alice said. "You can leave now. I need to shave all my bits and pieces."

"What?"

"Hey," she said. "I may never get another chance. I'm going for it."

"Need help? Can I stare? Anything?"

"Out," she said.

A few minutes later, she walked into the kitchen with only a towel wrapped around her, holding a tube of antibiotic ointment. She sat in a kitchen chair and leaned forward, exposing her back.

"Do me," she said.

Mason took the ointment and applied it liberally to all the wounds on her back. Then he had her sit up straight and put the ointment on the shoulder wound.

"Alice, I don't like the looks of that wound."

"I know. I looked at it already. Mason, you need to find an ice pick. Then, see if the stove works and boil water to sterilize some tea towels. We need to open this wound so it will drain. If it seals over on the outside and keeps the infection on the inside, I'll never find out if you can ring my bell. If there is a gas burner, sterilize the point of the ice pick in the flame. If not, put it in with the towels and boil it."

Mason held his hand out to her. "Hey, slow down. Who is the Boy Scout here? Are you sure this is what you want? That's going to hurt a bunch."

"It has to be done, and I am not looking forward to it." She put her hand on his arm. "Be strong for me, Mason. When I faint, just finish the job while I am out."

Mason found an ice pick in a drawer under the countertop. Tea towels were in a deeper drawer. He found a large pot and filled it with water, and set it on the burner. The towels went into the pot of water, along with a couple of steak knives that were really sharp. Then they waited. It took an ungodly amount of time to bring the water to boil. It seemed strange, given the amount of dirt they had been in, but he washed his hands with soap to make sure he was clean. When the water was boiling, he turned off the burner, and they waited for the water to cool. Once he could stand to touch the hot water, he drained it off and wrung out the towels. He was as ready as he would ever be.

Putting everything close at hand on the kitchen table,

he turned and took off his belt. "Let's get this done," he said.

Seeing him take off his belt, she said. "Mason, this is not the time..."

He pulled down her towel and put the belt under her breasts, then around the back of the chair. It was just large enough to buckle. When he had her fastened to the chair, he said. "Just in case you faint."

"Oh," she said. "I thought..."

"I know what you thought." He put one hand behind her head and kissed her while lightly brushing her breasts with the other. "I'll take a rain check."

"Dammit," she said. "I feel like I am in a bondage movie."

The front of the wound was about the circumference of a nickel.

He took one of the steak knives and flicked off the scab on the front, then did the same for the back of the wound. When he did this, she hissed through clenched teeth, her hands balling up the bath towel in a death grip. Working quickly, he started pushing on the puncture wound and blood and puss came flowing out. The second time he squeezed, she went limp. Then it got awkward.

With her head slumped forward, he was afraid she would block her airway, so he let her head roll back. That didn't work either, so he finally just supported her head with his shoulder.

"Why in the hell didn't I lay her down for this?"

Finally, he had cleaned the outside and squeezed as much from the wound as he could. All the bleeding was red. He took a couple of tubes of ointment and covered the front edge of a towel with it. Using the ice pick—again, a poor choice for the job at hand—he forced it into the wound, hoping to coat the insides with the antibacterial ointment. He did the same for the back. When he was done, he scrubbed her with the sterile towels.

Using some gauze pads he'd found in the bathroom, he covered them in ointment and covered the wounds and taped them down with Band-Aids. If there was adhesive tape around, he could not find it.

When he had done everything he could think of, he fished the syringe and needle out of the container he'd boiled water in, assembled them, and gave her another shot of antibiotic.

She was still out, so he unbuckled her, picked her up, and put her in the bedroom. She looked like she was sleeping and he hoped the sleep would help her.

Judging by the shadows outside, it was about midday. Another day was lost, and they were not moving. It was not a good plan, but the only one they had. He hoped this place would be overlooked. At least there was a back door.

Mason took a slow stroll outside and around the house. Someone had gone to a lot of trouble to conceal the utilities that served the house. He found a water tank slightly up the hill behind the house. It looked like it was spring fed. Next to it, he saw several straight poles that went up high enough to clear the adjoining foliage of the trees. Looking at the cable that came down one of the poles, he surmised there was a solar array up there that would only be visible from the air.

He paused again to look at the dead dog. A desiccated carcass hooked to a chain. He hated to see anything suffer and figured this dog had starved. Which brought up another thought. Whoever had owned the house had taken great pains to ensure their survival. Then something must have prevented them from coming home. Maybe just bad luck. Mason would rather be lucky than good any day of the week.

IT WAS NEARLY dark when Mason heard Alice's soft footfalls as she came down the hall to the kitchen. He had found canned soup, and it was about ready to eat.

She came in and gingerly sat down in the same chair she'd been in before. "Did you finally catch that squirrel? I'm starving."

"Chicken noodle soup. It's good for you," Mason said.

He put a bowl in front of her. "Crackers?"

"Of course."

Since her left hand was in her lap, he crushed the crackers for her as she stirred them into the soup. She didn't make any comment until she'd finished two bowls.

"I stopped by the bathroom and looked at my shoulder. It's sore but not too bad. I don't feel like I have a fever. You do good work."

"It must not have been too bad because you went to sleep."

"If we need to, I should be good to go. I know you want to keep moving. This is a good place, but it's too good to last, isn't it?"

Mason looked at her and shrugged. "Tomorrow morning, if you're up to it. If Tolliver was correct, there is another large group of people coming this way. They should slow down when they hit Springfield. It would be foolish to think we would be overlooked."

"I may need some help getting dressed," she said. He could see her eyelids were getting heavy and she could barely stay awake. Just when he thought he'd better catch her as she nodded off, she straightened up. "This cabin belongs to a survivalist, or at least a 'prepper,' right?"

"Looks like it," he said.

She looked at him. "Where is the gun locker?"

Mason looked at her with his mouth open. "Well damn me for an idiot. I swear I've lost my mind since this whole thing started. That should have been the first thing I thought of."

He picked her up and took her back to bed. "Get some sleep. If there is a locker, I'll find it."

"Wake me up when you come to bed," she yawned, already closing her eyes. "I owe you a rain check."

Right.

It took him an hour of pounding on walls and remembering the earth home, stomping on the floors, but he finally found it. In the dimly lit hallway, he found a piece of paneling that looked loose. He put the point of the K-Bar under it and the panel came away revealing a small closet-like space. The room was full of weapons and ammunition. He took a couple of M-4s, a small survival knife that was more like what was issued by the Navy for their aircrews, and as much of the ammunition as he thought they could carry. He found a few backpacks and clothing in olive drab. It was not army surplus camos, but the coloring was perfect for this area. Changing into a new set of clothes and filling his pockets with essentials, he found the smallest sizes and took them into the bedroom. When he dropped them on the bed, Alice didn't even twitch. *Rain check. Right.*

When he opened a box on the floor, he found it full of dried food in pouches, plus water purification tablets. Along with this was a decent field first aid kit and medicine for diarrhea, stomach cramps, and pain medication. He started tossing stuff out of his pack. The clothes in his pack could stay behind. This was a major find.

When he'd placed the weapons they were going to take next to the front door, he went back and closed up the paneling. Maybe they'd come back this way. Maybe no one else would find the weapons cache. Maybe.

Mason stood looking at the lumpy couch, thinking about joining Alice in the bedroom. But he knew the comfortable bed would make him sleep too soundly. He didn't give any thought to Alice's invitation. Well, not much. Besides, he still didn't trust the serene landscape outside. He could feel danger like a giant spider crawling up his back. It was coming. He rolled himself in a blanket and went to sleep on the couch.

TWENTY

MASON WOKE on the sixth day after the whole mess started. His view out the front window told him it was dawn, although the cabin was surrounded by so many trees that it was shrouded in darkness. He unwrapped himself and went to the windows, looking for any movement outside. Finding none, he went toward the bedroom to check on Alice. Hearing the toilet flush, he diverted to the kitchen to see about making coffee and organizing some kind of breakfast.

He could tell when she entered the room and felt her move up behind him. She hugged him from behind and held herself close to him. When she didn't break the embrace, he asked, "How do you feel?"

"Good. Sore, but good."

He reached into his pocket and pulled out two of the painkillers. As he handed them to her, he said, "Found some pain medicine."

She took them and put them in her pocket. That's when he noticed she had on pants and shoes. He had already felt she didn't have a top on.

"Later," she said.

"I have coffee going."

"Later."

She turned him around, raised up on her toes, and kissed him full on the mouth. After checking his tonsils for a while, she said, "You didn't come to bed last night. Just what does a girl have to do to get laid around here?"

He laughed as he held her body tightly to him. "You wouldn't have known it, even if I had come to bed."

"You passed up a chance to do wild and depraved things to an unconscious and"—she batted her eyelids at him—"voluptuous woman?"

Looking down at her, he brushed a wisp of hair off her forehead. "I think you must be feeling a lot better. Look, Alice, when that time comes, I want you to be conscious, alert, and well aware of what is going on."

"There is only one problem with that, Mason. If you keep putting things off, there may not be a tomorrow. Our future does not hold a lot of promise right now. We may not live long enough for things to be perfect."

"Alice, I promise to do my level best to make sure we have enough 'tomorrows' to make it happen. Besides, that is a huge incentive. I really, really want that to happen."

Mason left the room for a moment and came back with an olive green tee shirt. He handed it to her, saying, "Not that I don't like the scenery."

He helped her put it on. It was baggy but would be comfortable. He even tucked it into the new cargo pants she was wearing, letting his fingers get sidetracked enough to bring a startled gasp from her. Rummaging around in a drawer, he produced a pair of scissors and proceeded to cut off the bottom of the pant legs where she had rolled up the cuffs. He laid an extra 1911 .45 on the table, along with the survival knife he had found the evening before and several loaded clips for the .45.

"From now on, don't go anywhere without these."

She looked at him and said, "You found the gun locker. You have very nice hands, you know?"

Mason grinned at her change of subject. "More importantly, I found medicine, travel food, a couple of packs for all the goodies, and a couple of rifles. And..." He paused dramatically. "I found a map of the area. I now know where we are going and how to get there."

As she was listening to him, she sat down at the table. "That's my man. Now I need the coffee, and you can feed me. I don't suppose you found any cigarettes in there, did you?"

"Sorry," he said with a grin. "You quit, remember? Look, I need to walk the perimeter again. Can you manage?"

"Well," she said with a groan as she got up. "There goes Queen for a Day."

HE WAS on his second circuit and standing at the back of the house when he heard a noise out front. Going to the corner of the house, he peeked around and saw a woman approaching the house. The remnants of what used to be a dress hung from her body, and she was carrying a satchel and wearily pulling a little wagon with two small children parked inside, covered with blankets. The noise he heard was the wheels squeaking as they turned.

Mason stepped out from behind the building and said, "That's far enough."

The woman stopped a moment staring at him. It was clear from the way she looked that she was exhausted. She looked at the kids and then continued toward the house.

"Go ahead and shoot us if you want. We're half dead anyway."

Mason saw she was looking at the house when she said that and turned to find Alice on the porch. Alice was waving the woman forward.

The woman stopped at the steps and collapsed more than sat on the ground. "I'm Jennifer Boudreaux, and these are my kids. If you have any food to spare, they are really hungry."

"Look," Mason said. "We can offer you some food, but..."

Jennifer looked at him and said listlessly, "I know your voice. We've met, I think. The night of the explosion."

"Really?" Alice said.

She helped Jennifer stand up and had her kids out of the wagon and headed inside.

The woman continued talking as she walked wearily toward the house. "He had his hand on my tits, and I offered myself to him, hoping he wouldn't hurt us."

"He wouldn't have hurt you," Alice told her softly.

As the trio went into the house, Alice turned to follow them.

Mason said, "I'm going to scout around a while before we leave. See what you can do about feeding them."

As Alice went by him, she said, "Are you sure you are not gay?"

A few minutes later, Alice came out on the porch to find him standing in the same spot she had left him in. "I thought you were scouting around?"

"I had a feeling we were being watched and didn't want to leave cover."

"Well," she said. "If you'll go out into the yard and wave your arm over your head three times, you will get another surprise."

"I don't..."

With an exasperated groan, she went into the yard and waved. Within a minute, he could see people coming out of the woods. He thought this must be the group from behind the earth home because it was all women and children. There were at least twenty women with assorted children of all sizes. It was an eerie feeling, watching them file by him. They all had a haunted, faraway look as if they were shell-shocked. There was hardly any expression on their faces, including the children. And the strangest thing of all was their silence. He could actually hear their footfalls as they came up the steps and crossed the porch into the house.

"I think we've been evicted," Alice said as they both watched the last little boy turn and stare at them with large, round eyes before he turned and went into the house.

Mason looked at Alice. "You mean you're actually going to leave and not take care of all these refugees?"

"If you think I'm going to leave you here with about twenty grateful women, you have got to be out of your mind."

Mason smiled at her. "Alice, are you jealous?"

"Damned straight, I am. Actually, since you don't seem to like girls, I'm just being territorial."

"Besides," she continued. "They hardly seem human anymore. Maybe they can get their humanity back, but right now, they scare me."

"They've lost everything, Alice. Plus, they don't see any hope for a future. I can't say I disagree. They'll have a chance here and a little comfort, but who knows how long that will last?"

"We need to go, Mason. I don't like what this is doing to me. I used to like people, but now I don't trust anyone."

"Then we'll go in and say our goodbyes."

When they went inside, one of the kids had Alice's M-4 that Mason had left by the door; others were starting to open the packs he had left there.

Alice gently took the weapon from the child, and they both picked up their packs. Most of the people were just standing around, while some were trying to get the children to lie down and rest. They moved to the kitchen and found Jennifer heating food she had found in the cupboard.

Mason spoke first. "Jennifer, there is a lot of food stored here. If you are careful, it could last a long time. The water is still running, and there is electricity. Don't use the lights at night when someone could see. Do you understand this?"

Jennifer sat down, and her two children huddled around her. Tears made tracks down her dirty cheeks. "I don't know what to say. We've just been walking around waiting to die. We have women and children, but half don't belong to each other. I was lucky to find these two when Springfield went to hell. My little sister died protecting them. Every time we come to a group with men in it, we just get raped and beat up. Some of the women we meet are even worse. They don't want us around."

At the last statement, Mason saw Alice glance at him, chagrined. She had just expressed that very feeling.

Jennifer continued. "It's like everything has gone tribal. No one shares food or water. Anyone not in your group is the enemy."

"Look," Mason said. "Even if the people you are with move on, you stay here. Hide food and water...do whatever you have to do. If you can survive for thirty days, you have a good chance. Don't trust anyone. I know it sounds harsh, but you just can't."

The smell of food started permeating the house, and people started coming in the door. Alice stood and said, "Everyone stay out. You will all get fed. Kids first." She took a box of granola bars from the cupboard and handed it to one of the women. "Here, give these to the kids. If you have babies, there is canned milk that you can heat up."

She turned to Jennifer and said briskly, "C'mon, Jennifer. Get crackin' here. You're in charge. Pick some people, make them help you, and get everyone fed."

"I don't want to be in charge. I just want to rest."

"Would you rather they get violent and take everything away? They could hurt your children if you don't take charge and do it now."

At the mention of her children, they could see Jennifer visibly gathering herself.

"Okay," she said. "Okay."

She went out and got three more women to come in and help. Soon, it looked to Mason like everyone would have a good meal. When he got a chance, he pulled Jennifer aside and took her down the hall.

He showed her the panel with the weapons store behind it. "There are weapons behind this door. Can you shoot?"

"My dad used to take me target shooting."

"Arm yourself and anyone else you can trust, or at least that you think can handle a weapon. It is your decision. It might help, or it might make things worse. Get some food, get some rest, and then decide."

She went back to the kitchen.

"Let's go," Mason said.

"But...?"

"Let's go," Mason said again firmly.

"Maybe we should stay," Alice said.

He grabbed her as she started to go out the front. "Not that way. Let's go out the back. I don't want to walk that gauntlet and see those faces again. We'll have enough nightmares already."

THEY WALKED the lane until it came out to a blacktop road.

"Which way, Mason?"

Mason stood shouldering two packs and his M-4. Alice carried her M-4 by its sling over her good shoulder. "We go north. It would be easy to just walk down the road, but I think it would be too dangerous. We can walk a few hundred feet to one side and keep the road as a reference. North of us is a town called Dadeville. North of that is a place called Bona. That's where we hang a left and go to the lake. Fortunately, Sanctuary is on this side of the lake.

"Or," he continued, "and this is my personal favorite since I don't like roads, we can just strike out cross-country and save a lot of miles. It will be shorter but will probably take more time. I think that is the safest way. These little towns are full of country folk that have guns and know how to use them."

Alice asked, "Are you on a time schedule? I think as long as we have food and water, we should just take a stroll and use all the time we need."

They crossed the fence bordering the road and then headed northwest. It was slow going because they had a lot of fences to cross and skirted all the open fields, staying under cover. After walking a couple of miles, they noticed that ahead of them, the sky looked hazy. Mason put it down to clouds until they topped a small rise. Suddenly, that spider feeling was crawling up his spine again.

He stopped so quickly that Alice actually bumped into him from the rear. Holding a finger to his lips for silence, Mason backed them up until just his head would be showing above the crest of the hill. From his pocket, he pulled a small rubberized set of green binoculars.

Alice came up to him and asked in a quiet voice he could barely hear, "What is it?"

"Trouble," he said.

Alice unlimbered her M-4 and inched forward to the point she could also see over the hill.

At what looked like a small tributary to the lake, a huge campsite dotted the landscape. On the grassy slopes that went right up to the water, he could see small fires, he assumed cook fires, spread over at least a mile. They could see people sitting around, some walking about, and a few playing in the water. There were no children. The only armament he saw was held by men who looked like they were herding or guarding the huge mass of people. It was the same old story. The wolves and the sheep. Or sheeple, as some would call them.

On closer inspection, it looked like two camps. All the women were on one side and being guarded. The other side looked to be men. He saw some uniforms, some just wearing pieces of camouflage, but most were dressed like men in any hunting camp.

As they watched, two men came dragging a woman into their side of the camp. They were too far away to hear her screams, but she was fighting hard as they methodically ripped her clothing from her. She kept fighting until one of the men slapped her and knocked her down. Knowing he was too far away to do anything useful, Mason turned his head.

Movement from Alice caught his attention as she was inching her rifle forward and resting the barrel on a clump of grass. The magazine kept hitting the ground and altering her aim, so she finally rose up on her knees.

"Don't, Alice. You can't get them all."

"It's not that difficult a shot to make," she said.

"It is with that short-barreled brush cutter."

"I just need one shot."

When Mason looked at her questioningly, she said, "For her."

He stepped forward and kneeled beside her. His hand rubbed her shoulder. "Take it easy."

"Dammit. I don't want to take it easy! We can't just sit here and watch…"

It was over quickly, and the woman was left lying on

the ground. They could not tell if she was dead or unconscious. After a moment, the woman slowly turned onto her side and drew her knees up in a fetal position. Most of the women in the camp were standing and watching. Slowly, the crowd of women turned and went back to their cookfires.

"Maybe they were sending a message to the rest of the captives. Letting them know who was boss," Mason said. "That lady has a lot of spirit. As hard as she fought, she was probably a troublemaker."

Alice snapped at him. "So, that's how you men keep women in line? Cut them out of the herd? Rape and maybe kill them?"

He looked at her for a moment, shocked at the anger focused on him. "What I meant is that she won't let this kill her. She'll deal with it and then go on."

"That's how we're supposed to deal with it. Just say, 'Oh well,' then move on?"

Mason turned and walked away. *I don't need this crap!*

"Mason, stop."

He ignored her and kept walking.

"Dammit, Mason. Will you stop and look?" She nearly shouted at him.

He turned and was surprised that she was not looking at him. *So much for an apology.*

"How far is it from where the bad guys are to the cabin?" she asked.

Walking away, he answered over his shoulder, "About two miles, same as us. Why?"

He was startled as she went jogging by him, retracing their steps back toward the cabin. Curious, he walked to the crest of the hill again and scanned the camp with his binoculars. Several dozen men were arming themselves while a lone man was talking to Stark and pointing back toward where the cabin had to be. *Well, hell!*

He retrieved Alice's pack and followed after her. The dangerous spiders were jumping up and down on his back like monkeys gone berserk.

TWENTY-ONE

MASON CAUGHT up with Alice within a few hundred feet, reached out and grabbed her by her collar. "Stop a minute and listen to me."

She turned and fought him so hard he was surprised she didn't pull a knife. Finally, he caught her arms and shoved her away, just to get some space between them.

As he stood watching her try and catch her breath, he said, "Was that fun? You're bleeding again. What in the hell is the matter with you?"

"I'm going back to try and help those people at the cabin. You can go on north to my father's beloved Sanctuary, which he never got to use, and avoid this whole mess. I'm sure you don't want to get involved in a losing cause, Mason. I know this does not make sense to you. There might be fighting involved, and it goes against your rules for survival, but I'm going anyway. Maybe I can make a difference."

"Well, it has only been a few days," he said in a defeated voice. "I thought it was time enough for you to get to know me. I guess you just can't get to know someone in that amount of time."

He shook his head. "I guess we were just too good to be true."

She stared at him like he'd just grown two heads and then started running again. He caught her, avoided a head slap, grabbed her, and physically pointed her east. "About a hundred yards over there is the blacktop road. It will be faster."

They made it to the road, and he held the fence wires apart so she could get through. As they jogged south toward the junction that was close to the cabin, he went by her and said, "You don't know shit about me."

THEY JOGGED IN SILENCE, saving their breath. Neither was used to running like this, especially carrying heavy packs. Finding some source of energy, Alice kept trying to speed up the pace, and Mason kept stepping in front of her to slow her down. He knew, considering the terrain, that they had an advantage. From what he could tell, the raiding party didn't look all that motivated, and he doubted if they would run hard. Besides, he was sure they would want to enjoy the women once they got there, and running a hard two miles over broken terrain was not the way to do that. It would be easier if the men were preoccupied with the women. He wouldn't worry about getting to the party late, except for the children. He was willing to bet they were expendable to this bunch.

Mason figured they had made good time when they finally came down the lane and into the front yard of the cabin. There were kids playing outside that looked up, startled, and several women were sitting on the porch. The scene looked pleasant and normal. He hated to burst their bubble.

One of the women turned and yelled into the house. The Boudreaux woman quickly stepped out and then came to meet them.

Alice was already shooing the kids indoors when Mason spoke, trying to catch his breath. "Jennifer, we have trouble coming. Did you arm any of the women?"

"No," she said. "A couple of men showed up, though. They seemed to be okay and were armed already. We gave them extra ammunition."

Mason turned and said, "Alice, I don't suppose you'd consider taking these people and cutting out of here?"

"Alice?"

He saw her staring at a man that had come out on the porch.

Alice shouted at the man. "Kirk? My god. You're alive?"

Mason watched as Alice ran to the man and fairly leaped into his arms. *Well, hell.*

As he brushed by them, they were kissing and, since she was short, naturally the guy had to hold her up by her ass. *Swell.* Mason felt emptiness inside and a sudden knot in his stomach that wouldn't go away. *So much for quickie romances.*

"If you two lovers can find the time to stop swapping spit, we've got work to do."

Ignoring the scathing look she gave him while she struggled to get out of the man's grasp, he continued, "You need to fort up inside and pass out some weapons to the rest of the people."

Once everyone was inside, he turned to Alice again.

Her eyes were large, and she looked like she wanted to say something, so he quickly started speaking again.

"Look, you don't have time to play with your boy toy right now. Keep everyone down. Put the kids in the hall. They will be safer there. The walls of this cabin are thick and should stop anything from their light-caliber assault weapons. Hopefully, when they get through me, you'll take them by surprise and be able to make a stand. Let them get close, then give them hell."

She grabbed his arm. "Mason, please stop. What are you going to do?"

"Why, Alice," he said as he was checking his weapons and ammo clips. "I'm going to go out and do what we men do. I'm going to kill some people. It didn't look like they were taking any women along, so I won't have a chance to rape anyone. I guess I'll have to miss that particular fun. Your mind can rest easy on that one.

"Besides," he said. "You have everything you need right here. It looks like you and your lover boy found that fire you were missing."

"Mason, it's not what you think."

He interrupted before she could say anything else. "What I see with my own eyes is exactly what it is, Alice. There wasn't a lot of room for misconceptions."

Kirk grabbed Mason by the shoulder. "Look," he said. "You can't talk..."

Mason interrupted. "I've been told you are some kind of hotshot Army Ranger with a body of steel and one hell of a fighter. If you want people to keep believing that fantasy, you'd better let go of my arm, shithead."

The man's hand came away from Mason's arm like he had just stuck it into something hot. Mason stared him down for a few seconds and then said, "I don't have time for this."

Mason continued. "Lieutenant Stark is going to be high on my list. If I can get him, the others might quit. If not, then maybe I can cut the odds down a bit." He looked at her bitterly. "In the meantime, see if you can get these women to defend themselves. You can't cover all the windows. Maybe dickhead can cover one of the windows for them."

Mason looked at them a moment, noting that the man still had his arm around her waist. "I'm still wondering how they found this secluded cabin. Any ideas on that, Kirk?"

"I wouldn't have a clue," Kirk said.

Alice reached out and pulled Mason back toward her and tried to kiss him. He turned at the last moment and gave her his cheek.

"Trying to compare?" he asked.

Alice stepped back with a loud gasp.

As he went out the back door, he heard, "Mason, wait..." Then he was in the woods and so angry he could barely breathe.

WHEN HE WAS out of sight of the cabin, he stopped to get his breathing under control. If he could not calm down, he'd be dead in a short amount of time. *Dammit! She pissed him off!*

As he stood for a moment, he shook his head, trying to clear his thoughts. The enemy was coming, and he was going to meet them. If the women and children at the cabin were to have any chance at all—even Alice and dickhead—he needed to cut the odds.

On the other hand, maybe he should just leave. Cut country and run. The girl he thought wanted him—hell, she said she wanted him—was back at the house with her old boyfriend. It didn't take them long to get reacquainted. Mason wished the guy was ugly. Real ugly. He wasn't. Big, tall, and looked like he could handle himself. And Alice? *Stop it. You're getting mad again.*

Mason practiced deep breathing as he walked toward the west for about five minutes, slipping through the brush and trees. Finally, he heard them coming. They were crashing through the brush like a bunch of cattle, calling out to each other like they didn't have a care in the world. Mason had hoped they would be all bunched up, but they were scattered all around with no clear formation.

Stepping behind a tree, he let the leading edge of men pass by. He raised the M-4, intending to fire into their backs, but couldn't do it.

"Hold it!" When he yelled that, he stepped back around the tree and changed his position. The raiding party had stopped in their tracks.

"Who's that?" someone yelled back. "What do you want?"

Mason had moved several feet from his first position. "You men are heading toward a cabin full of women and kids. I'm telling you to back off. You have enough women in your herd already."

The unidentified man laughed. "There's never enough, man. It's going to be a long haul, and we're using up women pretty fast."

Mason had moved again. "There won't be a long haul for you boys. If you keep on this path, you'll be dead."

A man stepped forward and said, "There is just one guy. Take him!"

Mason put a three-round burst right through the top button of his shirt. The man twisted and fell but didn't fly ten feet like in the movies. He moved again just as the group opened up, firing at the last place they had heard his voice. Rolling behind a fallen tree, he fired over the log into the raiders. Two more men were down before the group found his position, and as the log was being chewed up by bullets, he rolled into different cover.

He knew this could not last. He'd been really lucky so far. Men were trying to get around him on both sides. If that happened, he was done. Mason started backing toward a rocky bluff he'd seen and took cover in the rocks. His third clip was empty, and he didn't remember switching any of them.

Four men rushed the rocks before he could re-load, so he pulled the .45 and shot into them point blank. The last one turned and tried to run away, and Mason nailed him in the back. Sportsmanship be damned.

Mason was not in a good position. Although the rocks afforded good cover, and the raiders could not get to him, he could not go out. He was pinned down. Swapping his half empty .45 magazine for a full one, he settled down to wait. At least he had not heard any firing from the direction of the cabin.

WHEN MASON LEFT, Alice was left speechless for a moment. She suddenly realized how all this had looked to Mason. He had not known her long enough to know she was a demonstrative, hands-on person. She had gotten lost in the moment, thrilled that someone she knew had survived, especially after the loss of Mary Chen. The kiss was a huge mistake. Huge.

Kirk tried to pull her close, and she slapped his hands away. With her hand covering her mouth, she could not believe what she had done. Why was she even mad at Mason? None of this was his fault. Now, he was mad and would probably get killed. She picked up her rifle and started out the door. Maybe she could find him in time.

"Please help us."

Alice stopped at the door, looking back at Jennifer. "He's out there because of me. I have to go to him."

"No," Jennifer said. "Well, maybe. One woman to another? If you have something going with him, and then he sees what you did with the new guy? He may not come back."

She continued. "Regardless, he's out there because in his mind, it is the right thing to do. He is buying us time to get ready to defend ourselves and our kids, and we don't know what to do. Please. Help us."

The Alamo. "Well, shit," Alice said.

"Yeah, it's that kind of world, isn't it?"

Alice gave a resigned sigh. "Okay, let's empty out that storage locker and get every gun loaded. We probably don't have long." Tears came to her eyes when she said that.

"Kirk, go out front and make sure no one sneaks up on us from that direction."

He smiled at her. "Maybe I should stay here with you."

"Wrong, Kirk," she snapped at him. "You don't stay

with me. There *is* no us. There is no we. Now, get to work."

"That's alright," Kirk said. "I can wait. He won't make it back anyway. There are too many of them."

She stared at his back as Kirk walked out of the house. "Now, just how does he know that?"

Alice turned back to the matter at hand. "Jennifer, get the kids into the hall or maybe into that storage room when we get it emptied. Then we'll put people at each window and wait. It's all we can do."

Within five minutes, they had it all done, the kids in the safest spot possible, and the adults were waiting at the windows. Alice placed most of the firepower on the west side. More than likely, that's where all the shooting would come from.

There had been a lull in the firing off to the west. Then it picked up again in full fusillade. Alice stood looking toward the west with tears running down her cheeks, silently praying for Mason.

A FLICKER of movement caught Mason's attention, and as he turned toward it, they rushed his position from three sides. He emptied his .45 and tried to re-load. Rock chips were flying all around him, and he had the crazy thought that he would have more wounds than Alice. He caught a bullet on the hip that spun him to one knee. As he came up with a full load in the pistol, he felt another blow to his shoulder. He looked up and saw more men rushing toward him, and he was firing.

His pistol empty, Mason threw it at the nearest man, making him duck and swerve away. Pulling his Ka-Bar fighting knife, he stumbled over the rocks and met them head-on. They didn't expect an attack. In their minds, he was supposed to run, or just die.

Mason was into them before they could react. He was taking a deadly toll with his heavy knife. There were too many men close to him and they were getting in each other's way. The men not in the fight could not fire at him for fear of hitting their comrades. Finally, someone got a clear shot at him and he felt a blow to the head and went to his knees. Struggling, he made it to his feet.

Mason could not tell how many places he was wounded. He knew it hurt to move and could barely see. Still holding his knife, he used his left hand to wipe blood from his eyes.

He meant for his voice to be strong, but it was not. Looking at the men circling him, he said, "Come on. Let's finish this."

Lieutenant Stark stepped out in front of him. "Look at him, men. This is the famous Mason Law. They call him a Shepherd, whatever the hell that is. He doesn't look so dangerous now."

One of the men said, "I know about twenty men who would disagree with that. If they were alive, that is."

Stark turned to the man and snarled, "Shut up, Peterson." Then he pulled a knife from his belt. It was a fancy, curved blade. All stainless steel and shiny.

"I think we should just gut him right here and leave him for the dogs to clean up," Stark taunted Mason.

Mason looked at him with tired eyes, holding his black, leather-handled fighting knife point down by his pant leg. "You are a coward, Stark. You need to accept that. No matter how hard you try, you can't change it."

Mason got what he wanted. Stark gave an enraged

bellow and charged Mason with his knife held high. Mason simply stood his ground. At the last moment, it took all his strength to block Stark's downward strike with his arm. Mason's heavy-bladed knife parted Stark's shirt like butter, and the blade went up under his sternum, slicing into Stark's heart.

The momentum of Stark's charge carried them both backward, and they both went down hard, with Stark on top. Mason felt another blow to his head, and he struggled with Stark's weight a moment before he passed out. Neither of them moved.

THE MAN NAMED PETERSON, who had spoken to Stark, walked over and looked down on them. The point of Mason's blade was sticking out from Stark's back. One of Stark's hands had driven his fancy knife into the ground. As he watched, the other hand grasped at the soil beneath it, then slowly relaxed.

Peterson shook his head. "There lies a man, boys."

One of the other men replied, "Which one?"

"Well, Red, I sure as hell ain't talking about Stark."

Red thought a moment. "We need to get moving. Those women may have run off by now. They'd be hard to find out in this brush."

Peterson had already made up his mind. He was thinking about the girl that had been raped that morning. After she was assaulted, she'd lay for a minute crying, and then she got up and went to the water to clean herself. When someone laughed at her, she gave them the finger. She had a lot of fight left in her, and he was going to try and talk her into leaving with him. If they were to survive, he needed a partner with a lot of attitude.

"I ain't doing it, boys. I gotta bad feelin' about this here. Think I'll do like the man said and go take care of what we have. We don't need any more. There's been enough killin'."

"Hell with that," Red yelled. "We're going to finish it."

Peterson smiled over his shoulder as he walked away, not quite turning his back on Red. "Your funeral."

THE FIRING HAD STOPPED, and it was eerily silent outside. As she stared out the window at the surrounding woods and brush, she had trouble seeing and there was a huge lump in her throat. She just couldn't see Mason as being dead. But, on the other hand, she knew he would still be fighting if he were able. She constantly berated herself for sending him off mad.

She was just thinking they would be ok, that maybe the raiders had passed them by when one of the women standing by the window next to hers thought she saw something moving.

"Everyone hold steady," Alice said. "Let them get so close we can't miss. Don't fire unless I tell you to. Look at the side of your weapon and make sure the safety is off. Jennifer, you have an older M-16, so pull the charging handle back. Everyone set?"

A group of men walked casually into the clearing. Alice quickly counted fifteen. They stopped a moment, looking around, and then started advancing toward the house. She could hear someone crying in the other room. One of the kids sneezed in the storeroom.

Alice waited. When one of the men put his foot up on the back step, she calmly said, "Fire."

The first man was literally blown off the porch, and she thought everyone must have aimed at him. A few of the men fired at the house and were cut down. But Alice could see it wouldn't be enough. The men at the rear of the group started methodically firing through the windows and she was aware of two women that went backward onto the floor. Alice and Jennifer were the only ones left firing.

Just as Alice ran out of ammo and was reaching for another magazine, the men in the clearing were suddenly attacked from both sides. The fire was pinpoint and devastating. In a matter of seconds, the rest of the attacking force was down.

In the silence that followed, a voice came out of the bushes. "Hello, the house. We're a couple of pilgrims looking to come in. We don't want to get shot doing it."

Alice was close to tears anyway but almost lost it when she recognized the voice of her father's longtime friend.

After she made sure everyone had heard and they would be safe, she yelled back. "Come ahead."

Seamus and Gretchen walked into the yard and checked over the bodies. Alice met them on the porch and slid crying into a hug from Seamus.

"I'm glad we found you, girl."

"It has been interesting," she said. "Thank you for helping us."

She then looked at the woman. "And, thank you."

"Gretchen," Seamus said. "This is the General's daughter, Alice Slade." He reached out possessively and pulled Gretchen to him. "Alice, this is Gretchen."

Gretchen extended her hand and, cutting a glance at Seamus, said, "After the last few days, it had damn well better be Gretchen McGill, but for now, it's Jennings."

They all laughed at that but sobered quickly.

Alice saw that Gretchen was clearly staking her claim, but didn't mind at all. Seamus was an old friend. As she turned and started filling her backpack and pockets with supplies, she saw Seamus looking around.

"Where is Mason?" he asked.

Alice didn't pause. "Out there somewhere. I have to find him."

"I don't understand."

Alice looked at them and could feel tears welling up in her eyes. "We were out and away from here and headed north to Sanctuary. We saw a raiding party heading toward the cabin. I forced him to come with me to try and save the women and children."

Gretchen looked startled. "I only know his reputation, but how do you force Mason Law to do anything?"

"The same way you would force that old codger standing beside you. I started back on my own. Mason loves me. He followed.

"Then I screwed up, big time," she continued. "When we came up to the house, an old boyfriend was standing on the porch. I was so surprised I went completely brain dead and ran up and kissed him."

She looked around her. "Where is Kirk, by the way?"

One of the women answered, "That guy you were all lovey-dovey with...?"

Alice winced.

"He ran away when the shooting started."

"Huh," Alice said. "Anyway, that kind of pissed Mason off."

Seamus just raised his eyebrows. "I'll bet it did."

Alice continued. "I didn't realize what it would mean for us, coming back. We got here ahead of the raiders, so he left us here and went to meet them. He said it was to even the odds, but I realized it was just to protect me. I may have killed him."

"Don't beat yourself up over this. It might have taken a minute to make up his mind, but he would have come back on his own. I know that." Seamus's face seemed to settle into grim lines. "That must have been one hell of a fight. That's one of the reasons we're here, to see what was going on. If that was Mason, and if these guys outside are what's left of the bunch we saw earlier, then it doesn't sound too good for him."

Alice shrugged. "I have to see for myself. I have to know."

Gretchen tried to reason with her. "Alice, there were close to fifty men. I know Mason is supposed to be good, but that's way too many."

"He could be wounded. He could be dying." Alice was near tears again. "Do you see any other choice?"

Before either of them could answer, one of the women came running in from the front of the house. "There's a bunch of people coming down the lane!"

Alice grabbed Seamus by the arm. "You guys get these women out of here. There are kids here, too. They don't deserve to die."

"No. We can't let you go it alone out there. It's too dangerous. If you die, then everything Mason has done will be for nothing."

"It does not matter. I love him, Seamus. I've only known him for three days, and I love him silly."

"Jesus," Gretchen said. "It took me five years and the end of the world to bring Seamus around."

Seamus continued with an annoyed glance at Gretchen, "Alice, we've been to Sanctuary. There is something else. I'm betting only you know how to open that door."

"I know how. My father told me. Look, I'm sorry, but you have to go."

"We can't leave you," Gretchen said.

Alice looked them both in the eyes. "Yes, you can. I'll join you as soon as I can."

Seamus said, "Okay, Alice. We'll see you as soon as these people are safe. If we don't catch up, we'll see you at Sanctuary."

She left them herding the women and kids out of the house and into the brush to the north. Taking a quick look around, she shouldered her pack, skirted the dead men in the clearing, and faded into the woods.

TWENTY-TWO

ALICE STEPPED around the bodies lying in the yard and thought about how surreal things had become. Not long ago, she was in a hospital emergency room fighting to save lives. Not long ago, while not perfect, she had a normal life with normal friends and a good future. Now she was looking at dead bodies with no more emotion than she'd give a tree in the landscape. Years ago, she had killed people in service to her country. At the time, they were the enemy. But this...? The world had gone crazy in less than a week.

Shaking her head, she faded into the woods heading west. She knew it was an awful chance she was taking, but just had to know. If Mason was dead, she would never forgive herself.

It could not be far from where the battle had taken place, because he had not been gone that long when the shooting started.

Getting there was almost an out-of-body experience; the freshness of the breeze through the trees, birds singing, and squirrels barking in the distance. She could have been doing a hike on a nature trail. On one level, she was scanning the area looking for un-friendlies, which included almost everyone. On a separate level, she strained to see any clue that she was getting close. She wandered through this innocent landscape for about fifteen minutes and then stopped on the edge of a small clearing.

Spread out before her, she could see bodies scattered everywhere, each one a macabre portrait of the fallen; some with arms outstretched, still holding their weapons, and some whose face became a rictus of pain and surprise. Most were dead, but a few were still moving feebly on the ground. The scene looked like the very thing that Mason had preached against from the beginning. The very thing he wished to avoid. A stand up and fight, devil take the hindmost, last-ditch battle with no winners. Now she understood. Too late, she understood.

Alice followed the trail of bodies toward a jumble of rocks against a sheer bluff. Here, there were many more bodies, some jumbled on top of each other. She took her time, nearly holding her breath, and looked everywhere, even at the edge of the trees. No Mason. Not knowing what had happened to him was tearing her apart. Did he crawl off into the brush like a wounded animal to die? Did his anger at her push him to follow the raiders back to their own camp? Oblivious to her surroundings, she slumped to the ground and cried.

"JESUS," Seamus said quietly.

"Joseph and Mary," Gretchen followed.

They had found out the party of people approaching

the cabin were peaceful. Strangely enough, some from each group knew each other, so they left the women and kids fending for themselves. A woman named Jennifer seemed to be taking charge. They were only a few minutes behind Alice when they stepped into the clearing.

Gretchen went immediately to Alice and squatted next to her, putting her arms around Alice's shoulders.

Alice said, "I can't find him, Gretchen. I can't find him."

Seamus took his time looking around, muttering under his breath. He finally joined the women. At a questioning look from Gretchen, he said, "I don't see him anywhere, so maybe he got away. It's not likely, though. That stand of rocks over there has a lot of blood stains. An empty rifle is there, along with his empty .45. It would be a place to make a last stand."

Alice sobbed when she heard that.

Seamus was still shaking his head in wonder. "Gretchen," he said softly. "I counted over thirty men dead or dying. I've never seen the like.

"I think I can piece it together," he continued. "It looks like he hit them where we first saw the bodies. They fought and lost some men until they got their act together. The firepower would have been overwhelming. He probably retreated to those rocks. That is probably his rifle with an empty magazine lying there. Some of the men near the rocks died from knife wounds, so I assume he ran out of ammo, pulled his Ka-Bar, and decided to make them earn it. Must have been something to see."

"So where is he?" Alice asked. "If he was killed, he should be here. No one would carry off his body. If he is alive, why didn't he come back?"

Seamus was frustrated. "All good questions with no answers, Alice. We'll keep looking. Maybe he crawled off somewhere."

They all heard the groan. Seamus whipped his head around and looked at a body a few feet away that looked so obviously dead, he had not approached it. It moved!

While the women watched, Seamus pulled his sidearm and walked over to check it out, fully expecting to have to put someone away.

He looked down past the man's head and saw a pair of eyes looking back at him. Instantly, he grabbed the body by the shirt and heaved it off. He found Mason lying in a shallow depression, still holding his fighting knife. He was covered in dried blood.

Alice and Gretchen were by his side in seconds.

Falling to her knees, Alice took charge immediately. "Don't move him! Let me see. Let me see."

"How can you see?" Mason's voice croaked. "You're crying like a baby."

"I can see well enough to tell you've been shot to rag dolls, so don't move." After a moment of checking him out, she said, "Dammit, Mason, you look like you've been through a meat grinder."

Seamus left the two women tending Mason and cut two poles about six feet long with his knife. He came dragging them back and said, "We have to move him. Right now. There may be more raiders hanging around."

"It will take a while for them to re-group." Mason's raspy voicc was barcly audible. "That's their fearless leader you rolled off me."

Seamus looked down at the body. "Stark?"

"Yeah," Mason said. "The damned coward didn't come for me until I'd already been wounded."

Seamus asked a question that had been nagging at him. "I thought your creed was to avoid conflict? Damn, man. What were you thinking?"

Mason tried to smile but failed. It just hurt too much. "There was not any other way to slow them down. I always said I'd rather be lucky than good. Today I was lucky. I don't know if it was good luck or bad. There were so many of them they got in each other's way. And, I never said I couldn't fight...just that I don't like to. I get mad and kinda go nuts. I don't like to lose control like that."

"How is that bad luck?"

"I lost my girl and tried to die for the second time. I'm still here. Bad luck."

Seamus left and found a couple of bodies that had their wounds up high and pulled their pants off. He put the poles next to Mason, and with the girl's help, threaded the poles through the pant legs, putting together a makeshift stretcher. It was not perfect, but would work for a while.

Gently, they picked Mason up and put him on the stretcher.

Seamus and Gretchen grabbed the ends. "There is a spring we found a couple of miles from here, at the bottom of a hill. It is hidden unless you fall into it... which we about did."

Gretchen said, "About did? Seems to me you're still wet to your knees."

Slowly, stopping to rest often, they made their way to the spring.

THE SPRING WAS a good hiding place for the short term. It was surrounded by trees and brush. The water came out of a shallow cave that went about ten feet back, and the floor was very dry.

Somewhere along the way, Mason lost consciousness. After checking him over again, Alice shook her head. "I think he is just sleeping. He is exhausted, and although his wounds are not too bad, he has lost a fair amount of blood."

Alice and Gretchen cut off his blood-soaked clothes and then with the pants from the impromptu stretcher, used them to make a pallet for him to lie on. After they had done all they could, Seamus and Gretchen went back to the cabin to find the medical kit they had left there and to check on the women and kids.

Mason had mumbled something about bad luck, but she didn't see any sign of it. She had never seen a man so lucky. Shot through with good luck came to her mind. It looked like a small caliber bullet had hit him in the head. Instead of penetrating, it had gone around his head just under the scalp. It was bloody but not too dangerous if they could keep infection out.

His hip had an angry red welt where a bullet had hit his belt, right at the hip bone, and bounced off. He had a piece of meat missing between his neck and shoulder that he'd never get back. It had bled a lot, but would be more painful than dangerous. He was also covered in nicks and scrapes everywhere.

Like my back after the explosion.

She took off her blouse and soaked it in the spring and then started washing some of the blood off him. The rest would have to wait. Her ministrations must have woken him, and she saw him watching her breasts as they swung freely above him, covered in a thin halter.

"Well, at least you're still interested."

"Even if they belong to another man, I still can't complain about the view," he said softly.

"You're an idiot. If things were normal, I'd tell you to buy a Lotto ticket."

He groaned as she pushed and prodded on him. "Somehow, I don't feel like I won the Lotto."

"The fact you can even feel this makes you the luckiest man alive."

"Some things I wish I could not feel, Alice. I thought we had something between us."

She collapsed on top of him, her head on his chest, soaking him with her tears. "Mason," she sobbed. "Can you forgive me for being such a bitch? I am truly sorry. I don't know what came over me."

"What happened to lover boy?"

Alice sniffed and wiped her eyes. "I told him to get lost, and he did. When the shooting started, he ran away."

She felt his hand behind her head, and then he was kissing her. When she pressed hard against him, he responded.

"Ow."

Through her tears, she said, "I'm sorry."

"Stop saying that." He continued, "It's been a hell of a week, hasn't it? It seems like a lifetime of hurt has been compressed into a few days. None of us are acting normal."

"Is it over yet?" she asked.

"No. Not even close," he said wearily. "There is not enough food in this part of the country to feed everyone that is here. The different factions and groups will start fighting each other soon. We don't want to be around for that. That's why we need to get to Sanctuary. We need a place we can disappear into until this madness levels out."

Alice pushed back into the small cave opening with him. Placing several weapons near to hand, she wrapped him up in her arms. "Rest. Tomorrow will be better. We'll be out of here soon enough. You'll see."

TWENTY-THREE

SEAMUS AND GRETCHEN didn't return until the next morning. They brought some blankets, water, and the medical kit.

"How is the patient?" Seamus asked.

Alice said, "He'll make it."

They went over to look at him. Mason started to sit up but was so stiff he could barely move.

"I'd wave, but I'm not sure I can move my arms," he said.

Seamus said, "You look like a human bruise."

"He is." Alice laughed. "He is also stiff as a board and can hardly move a muscle. If you have any painkillers in that bag, he really needs them."

"What's the matter with him?" Gretchen asked.

"I've seen it before," Alice said. "He is like an athlete that has played far beyond his ability or stamina. He kept fighting, even when he was out of energy. His body started drawing energy from his muscles. What he really needs right now, other than the pain meds, is about a gallon of some kind of sports drink. But, for now, we'll just have to do with salty water. Plus, he needs to rest for a day or so."

They held his head up and got the pain meds down him with a drink of water. Rolling him onto one side, they pulled the bloody clothes from under him and replaced them with a clean blanket. They put another on top of him.

Seamus started to talk to Mason, then stopped and grinned. Mason was already asleep.

SEAMUS AND GRETCHEN were huddled around a hatful of fire, stirring a concoction in a small skillet and talking softly with each other. Alice wandered over and looked at the mess. It didn't smell bad. Her stomach grumbled. She was tired of granola bars.

She sniffed and said, "What is that?"

"My special recipe," Gretchen said. "We got some powdered eggs, throw in some beef jerky, and then top it off with spam."

"There goes my diet," Alice said. "Let me know when you have some to spare."

"It's all for you and the stiff over there. We ate before we left the cabin. Those women were throwing together some pretty good stuff."

"Speaking of which," Seamus continued. "We're going to leave you for a while. We'll make sure you have plenty of weapons and ammo, plus food...and get your packs ready and all that. Just in case you need to bug out in a hurry. I don't think you'll need to worry right now. This place is pretty well hidden."

Alice paused from eating long enough to say, "Where are you going?"

"Well, you know we've already been to Sanctuary? We came back because we couldn't get in."

She waggled her fingers at them. "You need these. There is a hidden switch to activate the internal power. Once that is on, I have to use my palm print to get in. My father was a security freak."

"Well," Gretchen said. "Let's hope we can get you to Sanctuary."

Alice smiled at them both and then turned serious. "I told you that for a reason. One of the rocks next to the door is fake and actually made out of foam. If you use the butt of your knife, you can find it. Tear the foam away, and there is a switch inside, next to a screen."

She continued. "I am serious about this. If I don't make it, find me and take my hands."

Gretchen made a face. "Yuck."

Seamus said, "You make damn sure you stay alive, young lady. I'm not sure I could do that."

"So," Alice said. "Why are you leaving? How long will you be gone?"

"That cabin is a death trap now. Too many people have seen it. We got lucky and found a farm truck with a full load of fuel. What we're thinking, since we don't want to move Mason right now, is that we'll load up the women and kids and truck them up to the lake. It may take a couple of trips. If we run into trouble and we don't come back today, then you make your best way to Sanctuary. We'll meet you there if we can."

"That is dangerous, Seamus. What if the road is blocked or you run into one of the groups of people? You'll be sitting ducks in that truck."

Seamus laughed. “You are starting to sound like Mason.” He glanced at Gretchen, and she responded by reaching out to hold his hand. “We talked it over with the people at the cabin, and it is a chance we’re willing to take. Plus, we’ll be armed to the teeth. There were a few men with that second group that came in. We collected all the weapons from that raiding party and spread them out with the men and women. I don’t think we’ll be lacking in firepower.”

“Funny thing,” he continued. “The road is already blocked. The little junction in the road called Bona is blocked already. A group that calls themselves the Bona Boys are controlling that whole place. They let us through and back the first time, so I think we can make it again.”

Alice stood up and hugged them both. “Thank you. I don’t know what I would have done without you.”

Seamus chuckled. “I do. You’d survive. The General’s daughter could do no less.”

“Really?” she said sadly. “It does not sound like my father survived.”

“We won’t know about that for a long time, Alice. Don’t give up on him. He is a tough old bird. Anyway, we’d better get moving. We’ll see you before dark today or tomorrow early.”

Seamus continued, “Alice, you keep your head on a swivel. You’re well-hidden here, but you can’t count on it. Everything before now has just been a preview. I think the main attraction is still east of us and is heading this way.”

MASON AWAKENED and looked slowly around. Judging by the shadows, it seemed to be midday. Thinking about that, he supposed watches would still be working and would be for years, but he never wore one in the first place. Why he woke up thinking about the time was a mystery to him.

His stomach grumbled.

Alice immediately came into view. "Hey, sleepyhead. Sounds like you are hungry."

With an impish little smile, she kneeled down and kissed him on the lips. "Do you want food or me?"

"Uhh..."

"Boy, you sure know how to carry on your part of the conversation, don't you? It does not matter. I talk enough for both of us.

"Tell you what," she continued. "I'm going to feed you first, because you are going to need your strength."

While she was gone, Mason managed to sit up, stifling a groan as he did. He could not remember his muscles ever being so stiff and sore. Plus, he felt like he'd been knocked on the head again. Reaching up and feeling the long welt on his head, he didn't know how much more his head could take.

Alice returned with a metal camp plate full of food. "Gretchen cooked this up for us. It's pretty tasty if you don't worry about clogging your arteries."

"I don't think that is a big worry right now."

He took the plate and folding spork from her and started eating. Soon, he was wolfing down the food. He didn't realize how hungry he was. Now that he was sitting up, he could see Alice had a pot of water heating on the small fire.

When she saw him watching, she said, "This would

be easier if we had one of those little Coleman camp stoves. Maybe later, huh?"

"It would be hard to carry when we're on the run..."

Mason's voice trailed away as Alice stood and began stripping off her clothes. She dropped her blouse into the water and then took off everything else.

"I'd just bathe in the pool, but I don't want to spoil the drinking water."

His food was frozen mid-flight between the plate and his gaping mouth.

"Eat your food, Mason," she said to him with a smile.

Mechanically, he finished the food as he watched her using the wet blouse to wash herself. Mesmerized, he noticed her nipples were puckered and extended. As she washed her pubic area, he could see a definite five o'clock shadow appearing. *I'll bet that itches.* His brain was firing syncopated synapses as he watched her. A herd of elephants could have run right over them, and he would have never known it.

Finished with her bath, she brought the pot of water and her blouse and sat beside him.

"We need to get you cleaned up," she said as she kneeled naked next to him on the blanket. When she started to pull off the blanket that was covering his waist, he grabbed for it. She whisked it off him and grinned at his discomfort.

"Relax," she said. "I'm a nurse."

She cleaned his head wound and thoroughly scrubbed his body. By the time she was through, he was about as excited as he could remember ever being. She finally stopped and stood up. Wringing all the water from the blouse, she hung it up on a branch to dry. Turning back to Mason, she stood with her hands on her hips.

Mason watched her warily. In the short time he had known her, he knew that the unexpected was her norm.

"God, Mason, you look like you've been through a meat grinder."

He just nodded like a bobblehead doll. "So you said."

"As sore as your muscles are, I'll bet you can hardly move."

Mason was looking around for the blanket or his pants. "Yeah, I'm pretty stiff." *Bad choice of words.*

Alice stood over him, her feet on either side of his hips. He could see her eyes change to a deeper shade of blue.

"What are you doing, Alice?"

"Saying I'm sorry for the way I treated you."

"But you already did that."

"This will be way better."

As he watched her lowering herself toward him, he said, "You wouldn't...? I'm damned near helpless here." *Please, don't stop.*

"In that case, don't move. We don't want to start your wounds bleeding. Hey," she continued. "You are the one that said we couldn't do it until we had time for me to enjoy it. Well..." She chuckled. "I'm going to enjoy the hell out of this."

I think I'm in love.

She nodded her head and said softly, "I know."

TWENTY-FOUR

THEIR FRIENDS DIDN'T SHOW up that evening or the next morning.

Mason and Alice were up at daylight, fully dressed and ready to go. As he gathered all their gear and put it back into the packs, he stood and stretched. He smiled at Alice as he worked out a few kinks in his muscles.

"I feel pretty good this morning. It is a wonder what a good rest will do for you."

Alice gave a very unladylike snort and said, "You faker. I don't think you were sore at all." She yawned. "And if you got any sleep last night, I didn't see it."

Gunfire in the distance sent them scrambling for their weapons. Mason immediately started to move toward the cabin and the source of the gunfire.

Alice called to him, "Mason, don't go."

"We have to. It could be McGill. Sounds like someone got ambushed."

Alice gave a short scream, and Mason whirled toward her. She was standing rigidly, with a knife held to her throat.

"I really don't think you're going anywhere," Kirk said.

Mason could see he was having trouble holding the knife against a struggling Alice while trying to point his rifle at Mason. He finally shoved her away. The butt end of Kirk's knife caught Alice on the head, and she went down hard.

Mason caught himself and controlled his anger, playing for time. Looking for an edge. "Well, if it isn't dickhead. Is that the rest of your bunch attacking the cabin again? I figured someone had to be calling the shots around here. Things were just too controlled."

He could see the anger building in Kirk's expression as he took a step toward Mason. His rifle came up level.

"Yeah," Kirk said. "They are with me. They were always with me. I told them to finish it and load up the captives while I take care of you and look after my woman."

Alice stood up, holding one hand on her bleeding scalp. "I am not your woman. You'll have to kill me, too, Kirk."

"Doubt it," he said. "You liked me before, and you will again."

"No way. Different world. Different time. Never going to happen," she said.

Mason spoke gently to her as he watched Kirk. "Alice, why don't you step away? I think dickhead and I have something to discuss."

As Kirk laid his rifle on the ground, he kept his knife in his hand. "That we do, buddy boy. That we do. I'm going to enjoy this."

Why does everyone want to cut me? Mason shrugged and palmed his knife. "Then let's get to it, tough guy."

Kirk started some kind of kung fu dance, waving his knife around while Mason stood waiting quietly. When Kirk finally lunged forward, the sound of a shot echoed in the trees. Kirk dropped to the ground.

Mason looked at Alice as she lowered her pistol.

Alice shrugged. "I am sure you could have taken him, Mason, but I worked too hard getting you cleaned up. I didn't want his blood all over you."

Mason said, "Well, I don't think the staying clean part is going to work. You scared the shit of me."

She looked at him, trying to smile but losing way to tears. "I saw that movie with Harrison Ford. *Raiders of the Lost Ark*? I always loved that part of the movie where the bad guy brought a sword to a gunfight."

The sound of running footsteps brought Seamus hustling into the clearing just as Mason gathered Alice into his arms.

"Anybody need a ride to the lake?" Seamus asked, looking at the body behind them.

"What happened?" Mason asked. "We heard gunfire. Did they attack at the cabin?"

Seamus shrugged. "Yeah. Their first shot knocked a coffee cup out of Gretchen's hands." He grinned at them. "You don't want to see her pissed off in the morning without coffee. Besides, they were young and new to the fighting."

Mason hugged Alice closer to his chest. "We'll take that ride, Seamus. I'm really tired."

Seamus took off his bush hat and stood scratching his salt and pepper hair. "Son, if this is how Alice breaks up with old boyfriends, you had better keep on the straight and narrow."

EPILOGUE

MASON STOOD, holding a cup of coffee and looking at the woodland across the water from Sanctuary. Their defensive position was good. Hell, it was perfect. No one could see the entrance or see him unless they really looked hard. The beach leading down to the lake was all rock and gravel, so no tracks would lead to their door. Behind him, a huge boulder hid the entrance. Once behind it, a hidden flat panel made to look like smooth rock accepted a palm print to gain access. If the correct palm touched the panel, a pocket door slid open to the Sanctuary. It was high tech, or future tech on some things, and had cost millions. General Slade had it built to his specifications as a refuge for his family. Only one of his family had made it.

Alice, the General's diminutive daughter, was going to be pissed. In the three weeks since their arrival, she had pushed relentlessly to get everything in order. Of the survivors that made it to the door, everyone had a job. Mothers became teachers and kids were in school. Every item in the place became cataloged and evaluated. The place was as spotless as the emergency room Alice used to run.

The door behind him opened with a pneumatic hiss. Mason glanced over his shoulder. *Oh, shit.* Alice came out, went up on tiptoes and kissed him passionately on the lips. He held the coffee cup out with one hand and hugged her to him with his arm. After five minutes of this, she let him go. *She knew.*

She took the coffee cup from him and took a sip. Her face screwed up in distaste as she handed it back to him.

"So, when were you going to tell me?" she asked.

He didn't let her go. "I was just on my way."

"Liar."

"There is a memo on your desk?" Mason glanced down at her. *Wasn't buying it.*

Alice stepped away from him. "I saw your pack by the door. You were runnin' out of here like a thief in the night."

"It is morning," he said, smiling.

"Dammit, Mason. Get serious."

He sighed and looked away toward the forest. "Alright, I will. How many people do you have inside?" he asked.

She answered promptly. "We have thirty-one civilians, nine of them children. Plus, we have a crotchety old sergeant barely contained by his lovely lady, a beautiful nurse, and last, a man about to run away."

He ignored her sarcasm. "How many will Sanctuary hold?"

She sighed. He could tell she didn't want to answer. "About a hundred people, with supplies for up to a year."

"Well, there you go." He pulled her to him. "I can't stay here, Alice. It is a stainless steel tomb, and I'm going stir-crazy. There are more people out there, and they need help."

"We can't bring everyone here," she argued desperately. "We just can't."

"No, but we could bring in a few families. If we find them, a doctor or two would be good. We need skilled people for later."

Alice squeezed him tighter. "I can't talk you out of it?"

"Sorry, babe."

The door opened again, and two packs landed at their feet. Seamus and Gretchen marched out behind them, packed and ready to go.

He looked at them and knew he had to look like a frog that was just stepped on.

"Close your mouth, Mason," Alice said.

"What?" she continued. "You thought you were going alone? That is not happening. Since I have known you, there has never been a day you weren't beat up, cut, scratched, or shot. You need constant nursing. I'm going."

"If she goes, I have to leave, too," Gretchen said. "With Alice gone, that puts Seamus in charge. One week of that, and the peasants will revolt and kill us both."

Mason looked over their heads at Seamus. The sergeant shrugged. "I lost control a long time ago."

He shook his head and said to Seamus, "I should have tossed her ass out of that helicopter the first day."

Alice reached up and patted him on the cheek. "You'll be fine, dear. You can do what you want and go where you want. We're just your support group."

Yeah, right.

"Let's get this dog and pony show on the road," she said briskly.

Well, hell.

"Do I have to cook?"

A LOOK AT BOOK FIVE:
CHRYSALIS

AN APOCALYPTIC THRILLER THAT FOLLOWS A HEART-RENDERING TRANSFORMATION.

Colt Blaine had it all—a great job in scenic Springfield, Missouri, a new house in suburbia, a beautiful wife, and two wonderful kids. And then, in the blink of an eye, it all vanished.

With nothing to barter with for food, a downed power grid, and depleted fuel supplies in the Midwest, an apocalyptic nightmare has begun. Law enforcement and the National Guard are crumbling before organized gangs, and everywhere Colt looks, there are funeral pyres of desperate, starving people with no hope, nowhere to go, and nothing left to do—but fight for survival.

Still alive, Colt must traverse through gangs, sickness, betrayal, and death while finding love and loyalty in unexpected places and emerging an entirely changed man.

But what will become of his journey from despair to triumph in a dangerous new world...and who will he evolve into to get there?

AVAILABLE JULY 2023

ABOUT THE AUTHOR

Darrel Sparkman is an award-winning author of novels, novellas, and short stories. He's been included in three western anthologies, worked as a feature writer for *Saddlebag Dispatches* and blogged a short time for *Sundown Press*. His ideas come from a diverse past of serving as a combat search and rescue helicopter crewman in Vietnam and volunteer Emergency Medical Technician First Responder. He has worked as a professional photographer, computer repair tech, and was once part-owner of a commercial greenhouse operation and flower shop.

Darrel is enjoying semi-retirement and finally has that job that wakes him up every day—with a smile on his face.

www.ingramcontent.com/pod-product-compliance
Lightning Source LLC
LaVergne TN
LVHW030919080826
845145LV00013B/2968

* 9 7 8 1 6 8 5 4 9 2 9 6 0 *